by Henry Winkler and Lin Oliver

HANK ZIPZER

the world's greatest underachiever

A Brand-New Me!

To all the children around the world
who enjoyed Hank . . . this is for you.
And to Stacey . . . always—HW

For Henry Winkler, with everlasting gratitude
for letting me share Hank with you—LO

Cover illustration by Tim Heitz

GROSSET & DUNLAP
Published by the Penguin Group
Penguin Group (USA) LLC, 375 Hudson Street, New York, New York 10014, USA

USA I Canada I UK I Ireland I Australia I New Zealand I India I South Africa I China

penguin.com
A Penguin Random House Company

Doodles by Theo Baker and Sarah Stern

Library of Congress Control Number: 2009037775

ISBN 978-0-448-45210-4   10 9 8 7 6 5 4 3 2 1

by Henry Winkler and Lin Oliver

HANK ZIPZER

the world's greatest underachiever

A Brand-New Me!

Grosset & Dunlap
An Imprint of Penguin Group (USA) LLC

CHAPTER 1

Call me crazy, but when Ms. Adolf handed me the envelope that said HANK'S GRADUATION, I thought it was going to contain a note that said I was getting some kind of special prize. In my imagination, it said: *Because of your great Zipzer attitude and outstanding contribution to PS 87, we've chosen you to give the opening speech at your graduation. Congratulations!*

Or if not a speech, at least I thought they were giving me a statue of Principal Love that ran on batteries so when you switched it on, the Statue of Liberty mole on his cheek would light up and dance the hula.

But that's not exactly what the note said.

What it exactly said was this:

Dear Mr. Zipzer,

Unfortunately, you have not completed your community service requirement for graduation.

We are also notifying your parents that you have failed to fulfill this obligation.

Just reading that note alone made my stomach flip around like an Olympic diver jumping off the high board. But the note continued, with even more stomach flipping news.

Unless you complete your community service, it said, *you will not be able to graduate with the rest of your class. Please set up an appointment with Principal Love as soon as possible.*

So there it was. The one thing I had been looking forward to since I was born, which was graduating from PS 87 and getting out of there and leaving Ms. Adolf far, far behind, was kaput. Kaput . . . as in not happening. As in how did I get myself into this mess?

I just sat there staring at the note. I was so stunned that I didn't hear the bell ring, I didn't see Ms. Adolf pick up her roll book and leave the classroom, and I didn't notice that my best friends, Frankie Townsend and Ashley Wong, were standing in front of me, waiting for me.

"Community service?" I said to them. "Please tell me when anyone said anything about community service?"

"Uh, in the first grade," Ashley said.

"And in the second grade," Frankie added. "And the third grade, and the fourth grade."

"And five times in the fifth grade," Ashley continued.

"And they expect me to remember?" I said.

"And the last time they sent home a pink piece of paper that you were supposed to have your parents sign. Remember? It listed some choices for those who hadn't finished their community service."

"Like litter clean-up or graffiti removal or volunteering at the animal shelter. Is this ringing any kind of bell, Zip?"

"I think I'm hearing a tiny tinkle. It's a very small bell, but I'm sure it's there."

"Hank, did you lose that pink slip?" Ashley asked.

"I certainly did not, Ashweena. As a matter of fact, I put it to great use. It's protecting all of my favorite pieces of chewed bubble gum."

I reached into the pocket of my Mets jacket and pulled out a wadded up piece of pink paper and pulled it open as best I could. This wasn't easy because it was filled with little wads of A.B.C. Double Bubble. I'm sure you know this, but A.B.C. stands for Already Been Chewed.

I tried to read the note, working around the gooey splotches of hardened gum that covered most of the words.

"Look," I said to Ashley and Frankie. "It doesn't say anything about community service. It just says 'Dear ank.' And then down here it says 'nity serv.' And at the end it says 'wil graduate.'"

Frankie took the letter from my hands, very carefully, to avoid the A.B.C. parts.

"Okay, genius," he said. "Your gum wads are covering half the letters. It doesn't say 'nity serv,' which as far as I know is not English. If you look under the gum wads, you'll see it says 'community service.'"

Ashley, who was looking over his shoulder at the letter, chimed in.

"Yeah, and for sure it doesn't say 'wil graduate.' It actually says 'will not graduate.' See the not? It's right under that little clump of Juicy Fruit."

"Impossible. I hate Juicy Fruit. That's tropical-kiwi burst."

"Zip," Frankie said, handing the letter back to me. "The point is, you never took care of business and did your community service. So now your graduation is in jeopardy. You're toast, dude."

I stuffed the pink slip back in my jacket and walked over to my desk to pick up my backpack. As I slipped it on and started for the door, I realized that I had forgotten my math book, which would only have been the seven billionth time I had forgotten it.

Oh come on, brain. You have to help me out here. How about you start kicking into gear? I can't do this without you.

Frankie, Ashley, and I headed out of the classroom and down the hall, past the painted banner that had just been put up congratulating the graduating fifth-grade class. It said: MIDDLE SCHOOL, HERE YOU COME! There was a picture of each one of us fifth-graders, with our faces glued onto gold stars. The stars were pinned to a blue velvet cloth that I think was supposed to be the sky. I stopped and looked at my picture. I had my best Zipzer smile going in full force across my face, the one where I show my top and bottom teeth. I looked really happy. But that was when I still thought I was graduating with my class.

Suddenly, I felt a tap on my shoulder. I was so deep in thought, I jumped about forty feet in the air. When I landed back on the linoleum, I turned around to see Principal Love wagging his finger at me. His Statue of Liberty mole was not lit up, but he was grinding his teeth so much, it made his mole look like it was dancing the cha-cha. I hate when the mole dances the cha-cha, because it means . . . you're in trouble, Hank.

"Principal Love," I said. "I was just coming to see you."

"Really?" he answered. "That's funny because my office is in the other direction."

"I know that, Principal Love. I was taking the long way to give myself an extra opportunity to get some exercise. Kids today just don't get off the couch enough. Isn't that right, Frankie?"

"Yeah, we're total couch potatoes," Frankie agreed, giving Principal Love his famous one dimple smile.

"But not Hank," Ashley said. "He is one hundred percent committed to good health practices."

I flashed her a look that said, "Cool it, Ashweena. That's going a bit too far."

Principal Love wasn't buying one syllable of it. He was all business.

"Young man," he said. "Stop this chitter chatter instantly and accompany me to my office where we will discuss your future, or lack of same, the future being where you should go as opposed to your present direction, which is where you should not go, but you're heading there, anyway."

If you're having trouble following good old Principal Love, imagine how I felt. I didn't understand one word after "young man." When he talks, I feel like I need a translator from the United Nations.

Principal Love didn't even wait for me to answer. He spun in a very tight circle on his black Velcro sneakers and headed down the hall in the direction of the stairs that led to his office. I love that move of his, and I tried to imitate it, spinning around in that same tight circle. When I finished the spin, I was facing Frankie and Ashley. I stuck my hands out and said, "Ta-da!"

Both of them said the same thing at exactly

the same moment.

"Don't be cute, Hank. Just go."

"No problem," I said. "This is me, heading toward Principal Love's office. He and I are just going to talk this through, man-to-man."

"No, Zip," Frankie said. "He talks, you listen."

"I have things to say. Important things."

"Hank. Not now. Your graduation is at stake. So just shut it and do what he says."

The thing about Frankie and Ashley is that they worry way too much. Me, I don't worry. My grandfather, Papa Pete, always says, "Worrying doesn't make it better." And I couldn't agree more. So whenever possible, I try to limit my worry time.

But as I caught up to Principal Love, followed him into his office, and watched him slam the door closed behind us, I thought to myself, "Wow, this might be a really great time to start worrying."

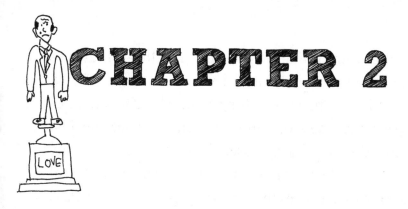

CHAPTER 2

"**Young man,**" Principal Love said before I had even put my butt in the chair across from his desk. "This is probably the last time that you and I will meet like this to discuss your inability to complete the tasks required of someone such as yourself that will allow you to leave the hallowed halls of a school such as this."

He looked up and without taking a breath, added, "And why are you still standing? Take a seat. Any seat. The red chair will do."

I knew that chair . . . my old friend, the red chair. I've sat in that chair for the last six years. I know exactly where to rub my jeans across its leather to make it sound like I had beans for lunch, if you know what I mean. I sat down and before I could get completely comfortable, Principal Love continued. He couldn't wait to have his words fill the room, and I thought the walls were going to pop like a balloon that was pumped with too much helium.

"I have been watching you, Mr. Zipzer, since your first day of kindergarten, and let me just say, the word impressed has never entered my mind. Other words have, however. Lazy, irresponsible, not living up to your potential, class clown, and impulsive . . . just to name a few. All these words help form an impression of a person who does not want to graduate, who is not on his way to graduate, and who in fact, may never leave this school."

"But . . ." I started to say.

"No buts about it," he interrupted. "The world of education recognizes those students who are willing to extend themselves through hard work, concentration, and . . ."

"But . . ." I tried to say. I mean, I really had to defend myself here.

"There's that but again," Principal Love said. "I suggest you open your ears and close your mouth and hear what I have to say, because what I have to say is what you need to hear, which you can only do with your ears and not your mouth."

"But, I . . ."

"No, Mr. Zipzer," he said pointing at me with his hairy, stubby index finger. I looked closely at it and noticed he bites his fingernails. Wow, I thought only kids did that. "Listen, don't speak."

I felt pretty good about my response, though. At least I got in two words. You definitely have to admit that's progress.

"Mr. Zipzer," Principal Love went on. "I know what you're about to say. I've heard every reason, every excuse, every wisecrack . . . all of which have brought you to this sad and bleak and embarrassing moment."

Oh, I *had* to answer that.

"B . . . b . . . b . . . b . . . b . . ."

He stood up suddenly, held up his hand, and just said, "NO! You will not make use of your mouth, lips, or tongue."

On the one hand, it was too bad that he wouldn't let me speak, but on the other hand, saying all those b's in a row made my lips buzz. At least they were having fun.

"As the records show, Mr. Zipzer, you have done exactly zero hours of community service."

Oh right. We're back to that again. I almost forgot why I was in here.

"But I can explain why, sir."

Look at me! I got a whole sentence out. Of course, it didn't help . . . but I got it out.

"Your explanations are of no interest to me, Mr. Zipzer. Here's all you need to know. You have exactly ten days to complete your required twenty hours of community service. What are your plans to accomplish that?"

I had no plans, but I did have a thought.

"Principal Love," I said with a big smile. "What is your favorite suggestion of something I could do to fulfill my requirement?"

I thought he'd be pleased that I was asking for his input. But it didn't quite work out that way.

"Good try, Mr. Zipzer," he snapped. "But this is something you should be in charge of, not me. It has to be your passion. What are you passionate about?"

"You mean community service wise?" I asked.

"What do you think we're talking about here, young man?"

Wow, that was a hard question. What was I passionate about, community service wise? Once

I volunteered at the animal shelter and held some really cute puppies. Until that little schnauzer with the white spot on his chest peed on me. That brought my passion level way down. And another time, Frankie and I collected litter on Rockaway Beach until we found a dollar and went off to buy ice cream sandwiches at the snack bar . . . which is also one of my passions. I like the ones that have three flavors of ice cream including strawberry.

"Hey, Principal Love. I do have a passion. Can I see how many ice cream sandwiches I could eat in ten days? Would that work?"

"Leave my office right now, young man, and don't come back until you've written out a plan to complete your community service. And keep in mind what happens to people who don't graduate fifth grade. Turn that over in your mind a few times. Perhaps that image will kick-start your wandering brain."

My brain wandered out of that office as fast as it could, and before I could stop it, it had wandered itself right into a list of what happens to people who don't complete the fifth grade.

If you're curious, turn the page.

CHAPTER 3

WHAT HAPPENS TO PEOPLE WHO DON'T COMPLETE THE FIFTH GRADE

1. You get to ignore the alarm clock and sleep as late as you want. How great is that!
2. You get to lie on the couch and watch TV all day. Wow, that sounds wonderful.
3. You get to eat pizza for breakfast, lunch, and dinner. Why didn't I think of that before?
4. You get to play video games until your thumbs fall off. Who needs thumbs, anyway . . . you wouldn't have to hold a pencil anymore.
5. You get to see your friends whenever you want and watch movies on the computer. Yeah, that's the life.
6. Wait a minute. What am I thinking? If I slept late every day, I'd miss the morning.

And I really like the morning, especially the smell of cooking waffles coming out of everyone's windows.

7. And about that all-day TV watching . . . come to think of it, it's mostly soap operas that are on, and everybody's yelling at one another . . . and if they're not yelling, they're kissing. Ick.

8. Pizza for breakfast, lunch, and dinner? Hey, I love pizza, but the thought of eating it three times a day every day is making me burp, and I haven't even had one piece yet.

9. And playing video games really gets boring after a while. And I don't want my thumbs to fall off. I like my thumbs. They really come in handy when you're giving a thumbs-up sign.

10. And about hanging out with your friends all day . . . well, that's not going to happen . . . they'd all be in school. That's where I should be!!!!!!!!!!!!!!!!!!!

So, let me ask you a question. Anyone out there got any good ideas for community service projects???

Freedom!

CHAPTER 4

Whoops. False alarm. You can stop thinking about community service projects for me now. Mr. Rock, great guy that he is, came to my rescue.

I had just pulled Principal Love's office door closed when Mr. Rock, who is the music teacher at PS 87, came strolling down the hall, carrying three clarinets, two saxophones, and a trombone. He could barely see out from behind all those horns.

"Hey, Hank," he said. His voice sounded pretty weird, because he was talking into the cone of the trombone. It sounded like he was a baby whale underwater calling for his mommy. "I really need your help."

"Sure, Mr. Rock. Let me take those saxophones off your hands."

I reached out and tried to remove the instruments from the tangle of horns, but Mr. Rock's fingers were wrapped around them pretty tightly.

"You can let go now, Mr. Rock. I got them."

"Please be careful not to let them drop, Hank. These are the only ones we've got, and the school has no money to replace them."

I took the two horns and followed Mr. Rock down the stairs to the music room in the basement, concentrating so hard on not letting them slip out of my hands.

"Can I ask you a question, Mr. Rock? Why are you carting all these horns around the hall? Not that there's anything wrong with that."

"These are the instruments that the band members were borrowing to practice at home," he answered. "I'm collecting them all, and I'm going to have to sterilize them, polish them, and store them for next year. It's a big job."

Bingo!

I don't know what you're thinking, but what I was thinking starts with the letters C and S and rhymes with *zammunity bervice.*

"Hey, Mr. Rock," I said as we approached the door to the music room. "If I helped you clean and polish and store the instruments, would you call that a service to our community?"

"Of course I would, Hank. You would not only be helping me, but also the students who participate in band next year."

"Great," I said. "Then I'm volunteering. Raising my hand. Signing myself up for the job."

"You know, Hank. This isn't a one day task. You'd have to come to me after school every day for at least a week."

"Now that you mention it, Mr. Rock, I'm sure that it will take just about twenty hours. Wouldn't you say?"

By then, we were inside the music room. Mr. Rock switched on the lights, laid the clarinets and the trombone down on his desk, took the two saxophones out of my arms, and put them on their stands. Then he turned to face me, and he had this funny smile on his face. Don't get me wrong. It was a nice smile, the kind that says, "I know what you're up to, young man."

"You weren't by any chance discussing your community service requirement with Principal Love, were you?"

"Funny you should ask." I smiled back. "That's exactly what we were discussing.

Correction. We were not discussing it. He was lecturing and I was nodding."

"I've nodded with him a time or two myself," Mr. Rock said with a laugh. "But I found it to be a great neck exercise."

That's the cool thing about Mr. Rock. He's not like other grown-ups who think all other grown-ups are so correct. He's willing to see things from a kid's point of view.

He stuck his hand out, shook my hand, and said, "This is our contract, Hank. You help me with the instruments, and I'll sign your community service form. You have to do the work, though."

"I will, Mr. Rock. I promise."

"Great. Do you have the form with you?"

"As a matter of fact, I do."

I reached into my Mets jacket pocket and pulled out the crumpled pink mess that was my community service slip. The gum wads were still there, of course. The thing about gum wads is that they just don't disappear when you want them to.

I flinched when Mr. Rock reached for it.

"I can explain," I said.

"No need," Mr. Rock answered, pulling his hand back without touching the paper. "I think I understand what happened. But you might want to stop at the office and pick up a new slip."

"Done," I said. "But can I just give you one small tip, Mr. Rock?" I pointed to a particularly large wad of purple gum that was smooshed in between a green wad and a pink wad. "This grape-raspberry burst Bubbletastic lasts the longest."

"I'll keep that in mind," Mr. Rock said.

With that, I bolted out of the music room and headed straight for the office to get my new community service form from Mrs. Crock. It felt like a three-ton hippopotamus had been lifted off my shoulders. I mean, one minute I was in a gigantic pickle (which I love, by the way). And the next minute, a Zipzer solution came flying out of my brain.

Sometimes it's great to be me!

CHAPTER 5

I walked home, and I promise you, I was taller. Or at least it felt that way. It's amazing what finding a solution to a problem can do for you. And I have to confess, the idea of graduating from PS 87 wasn't a bad idea, either. It was time for me to move on. To see what the future held. To take responsibility for my new life.

Whoa, just hold on there, brain. Take responsibility? I don't think so. Maybe I'll just stick with graduating from the fifth grade first.

As I hurried down 78th Street and crossed over Amsterdam Avenue, I saw Mr. Kim putting water in all of the flower buckets in front of his corner grocery store.

"Hi, Hank," he said. "How was your day?"

"Hi right back at you, Mr. Kim," I said, giving him a high five. "My day is looking better and better every minute."

"Then you should celebrate," Mr. Kim said. He reached over the flowers and grabbed a big bunch of something leafy and green with big, round, lightbulb-looking things at the bottom.

"Here," Mr. Kim said. "Have some bok choy. Enjoy."

"Wow, Mr. Kim. This is so . . . um . . . unexpected. And so organic. And so . . . what do I do with it?"

"Your mother will know."

"Uh-oh. That's a dangerous thought. Knowing her, she'll put it in the pot looking all nice and green, and then she'll add octopus suction cups and who knows what else, and it will come out all brown and slimy and stinky, like everything else she cooks. And if you ever see her," I added, "please don't tell her I said that."

Mr. Kim laughed. "It's our secret."

I tucked the bok choy into my backpack and ran the rest of the way to our apartment building. I even heard myself singing as I stepped into the elevator and punched ten. I don't sing often, and if you heard me, you'd know why. But this is what I sang.

I'm graduating . . . I'm graduating . . .

I never thought I would, but I am . . .
Graduating, yes, graduating.

Okay, I didn't promise you a good song, but it's my song, and trust me, it felt really good coming out of my throat.

When I burst through the door of our apartment, the first thing I saw was my dad, sitting in his boxers at the dining room table, staring at his computer screen, which was filled with columns of little irritating numbers.

"Hi, Dad!" I hollered. "I got some bok choy for you!"

You'd think he would have been happy. I mean, how many times in his life has he gotten bok choy for no reason at all? But my dad is my dad, and happy is not his middle name. You're probably not interested, but in case you are, his middle name is Whoopington. No kidding, it really is. Like the whoopee cushion but without the noise.

"You're late," was the best greeting he could muster up.

"But I have a good explanation."

Just then, my sister Emily wandered in from her bedroom, with her iguana, Katherine, draped around her neck like a scaly scarf.

"Don't tell me," she said. "You were look-ing for your math book which you couldn't find because it was in your backpack which you couldn't find because you had left it in the lunchroom where you forgot to get the change from the mac 'n' cheese lunch special which you dropped on the way to your table."

"I'm amazed, Emily," I snarled. "How did you know?"

"It comes with the territory," she answered, with her freckled nose up in the air. "When you're smart like me, you know these things."

"Well, I know things, too," I said. "Like your lizard is barfing on your sweatshirt."

Boy, did I get a good laugh when she looked at her sweatshirt with total panic.

"That's enough, you guys," my dad said. "You both have better things to do, and I've got to finish this financial report before five."

"That works out perfectly, Dad," I said, dropping my backpack and the bok choy on his recliner chair. "It'll give me a chance to hang out with Frankie and Ashley."

"They're in the clubhouse," Emily said. "And I want to come."

"You can," I said to her. "Just wait until tomorrow."

"But you guys won't be there then."

"You see? You do know things."

Without waiting for her answer, I ran for the front door. Luckily, the elevator was still waiting on my floor. I popped in, pushed *B* for basement, and was on my way. I couldn't wait to tell Frankie and Ashley the good news. We would all three graduate together, just like we had always planned.

I used the elevator ride down to the basement to continue singing my song. Wait. Don't put the book down. I will spare you this time. Just imagine someone singing my graduation song, who sings really well.

The basement smelled like its usual soap suds self, which meant that someone from the apartment building was doing a load of laundry. I could hear Frankie and Ashley's laughter from down the hall. I couldn't make out what they were saying, but it sounded like they were having a great old time.

"Hank Zipzer, reporting for fun," I said, poking my head into our clubhouse storeroom.

Frankie and Ashley were both sitting on the old flowered couch, with their feet up on two cardboard boxes that were labeled MRS. FINK'S SUMMER HATS AND MR. PARK'S VINYL RECORDS. I don't know why grown-ups save everything they don't want in cardboard boxes. It seems to me that the stuff just sits around for a hundred years, then when you go to pick up the box, everything falls out of the bottom. But the good news is, those cardboard boxes in storage make great footstools for our clubhouse.

When I walked in, Frankie and Ashley stopped talking. It was weird, though. It wasn't like they just stopped talking. I mean, they stopped short, like in the middle of a sentence. And then they both looked up and stared at me. I didn't know why, but the look on their faces reminded me of the way our dog, Cheerio, looks when I catch him chewing on my fuzzy plaid slippers.

"Wow, Zip!" Frankie said. "What's going on?"

I noticed that he took a piece of paper that was in his hand and stuffed it down in between the cushions of the couch.

"Guess who got his twenty hours of community service rolling?" I said.

"That's so great, Hank!" Ashley said. "You really gave us a scare for a minute."

Wait a minute. Was that her hand stuffed down between the cushions, too? Yes, it was. There was something going on here.

"What did you guys stuff down there between the cushions?" I asked.

"Nothing," Frankie said. "We were just looking for change."

"A person can always use some extra spending money," Ashley agreed.

"Guys," I said. "We've known each other since we were droolers. I can tell you're hiding something. So what is it?"

My mind was going over the possibilities. It wasn't my birthday, so it couldn't be a birthday present. It was too early for a graduation gift. I'm not a father, so it couldn't be a father's day card.

And I'm not a mind reader, so I had no idea what it was.

CHAPTER 6

Frankie and Ashley just sat there on the couch in our clubhouse like statues. It was so quiet, you could hear the dryer spinning down the hall and the pigeons making their little pigeon noises through the barred windows.

"Are you going to make me reach down there myself?" I asked finally.

"Zip," Frankie said. "It's a long story."

"So shorten it up to a sentence."

"I think we should start at the beginning," Ashley said.

"Well, I think we should start at the end. Just show me what you're hiding."

Frankie sighed, looked at Ashley, reached down and pulled out two pieces of crumpled paper. He held them out to me and I could tell by the look on his face that whatever those papers were, they were not gift certificates.

"How about you just tell me what it says? Unless it's really bad news, and if it is, you can stuff them back in the couch."

"It's good news and bad news," Ashley said. "Good news for us, and we didn't want to hurt your feelings."

I wasn't getting it. I mean, how could something that was good news for them hurt my feelings? They're my best friends. Good news for them is good news for me, right?

"Dear Mr. Townsend," Frankie began reading. "We are pleased to inform you that your application to the Anderson Middle School Gifted and Talented Program has been accepted. Congratulations!"

I looked over at Ashley.

"Mine says the same thing," she said. There were tears in her eyes.

All of a sudden, it hit me like a ton of bricks. I didn't get that letter. I didn't get any letter except the one from the school saying that the smell of old bananas was still coming from my locker and would I be kind enough to clean it out with a soapy sponge.

"Wait a minute," I said, a little confused.

"That means you guys applied to this genius school and never even told me?"

"We told you we were taking the entrance exam," Frankie said. "Remember? That Saturday when Papa Pete took you bowling and we couldn't go."

"Yeah, I knew you were taking a test, but I didn't know that test meant . . ."

I couldn't even think it, let alone say it.

"Wait a minute! Wait a minute! Wait . . . a . . . minute."

My mind was spinning.

"Are you telling me that we're not going to the same school? We've been in the same class since kindergarten."

"Zip, let me explain. There's more to it."

"Oh good. I know what you're going to say. That you got in, but you're really not going, because who wants to go with a bunch of geniuses, anyway. Phew, that's a relief."

"Hank," Ashley said. "It's a huge honor to get picked for the Anderson School. There are over 500 applications for only 184 seats."

"We can't say no," Frankie added. "And we'll still be able to see each other after school and on weekends and stuff."

"I know, I know, it's an honor and every-thing." I was really trying to be glad for them, but my emotions just wouldn't cooperate. "You're going to make new friends and have really hard homework and lots of it and me, I'll just be . . . where? Hey, where will I be?"

"You'll go to the regular middle school, whichever one you applied for," Ashley said.

"Who even remembers what I applied for?" I answered. "I just checked all the boxes on the form."

"So," Frankie said, "you'll probably go to MS 245 with a bunch of other kids in the class."

"Oh, thanks a lot. Me, Luke Whitman, and his pet slug. But that's okay, because you guys will be hanging out with your new group of Junior Einsteins."

"You're going to be fine," Ashley said.

"Yeah, Zip. We're best friends. That doesn't just evaporate into the ozone."

"See?" I said. "That genius school is already rubbing off on you. Now you're using words like evaporate and ozone. What's next? You're going to tell me my epidermis needs washing? Oh, that means skin, if you didn't know."

"I have an idea," Frankie said, standing up and putting his hand on my shoulder like nothing had happened. "Why don't we go to my apartment and watch the Mets game?"

"That sounds fun," Ashley said.

I could tell they were desperate to change the subject.

"You guys go ahead," I said. "I'm going back to my apartment. I have a lot to think about."

"Don't be like that, Zip."

"No, it's okay. I understand, really I do. It's just really hard to understand. Know what I mean?"

Suddenly, I felt like I was going to cry and I really didn't want to do that in front of them. They're my friends, and something good had happened to them. I should have been happy. On the other hand, my life as I knew it was about to change completely.

And if there's one thing I'm allergic to, it's change. *Uh-oh. I feel a rash coming on right behind my knees.*

CHAPTER 7

As I rode up the elevator, my heart was pounding. This was a lot of information to take in, and my brain was in a not-taking-in mode. I needed to be alone, to think, to work this out.

I took my key out of my jeans pocket before the elevator even stopped at the tenth floor. The moment the doors flew open, I was out and heading to our front door. Unfortunately, our neighbor Mrs. Fink had other plans for me. It seemed as if she was looking through her peep-hole waiting for me.

"Hank," she said as she stuck her head out her door. "What do you smell?"

"Nothing, Mrs. Fink. My nose is on vacation at the moment."

"Such a funny boy," she said with a laugh. "It's my cherry strudel. And it's calling your name. Can you hear it? Or are your ears on vacation, too?"

"As a matter of fact, they're on the same plane. Really, Mrs. Fink, I can't eat right now. I have some thinking to do. I hope you understand."

"Thinking is good," she said. "But eating is better."

I gave her a friendly wave as I opened my door. I was so determined to get to my room that I let the door slam behind me. I hoped Mrs. Fink didn't take offense. I'd explain it to her later when I came back for the strudel. But right then, it was room, sweet room that I needed.

I headed down the hall to my room and flung open the door. Oh boy. There it was. A sight I was definitely not expecting.

There's no nice way to say this, so I'm just going to come out with it. What I was staring at was my baby brother, Harry, or should we say, the bottom part of my brother, Harry. And when I say bottom, I mean bottom. He was lying on his changing table, and my mom was holding his legs straight up in the air, changing his diaper. And the aroma that came from that exact direction made the hair in my nose curl up and down so fast, it made me sneeze.

"Bless you, Hank," my mother said.

I couldn't even get a word out, I was gagging so hard. How do mothers do it? Maybe when you have a baby, your nose stops working for a year or two to let you change diapers without fainting. That had to be the case because, otherwise, my Mom would be on the floor constantly.

"Mom, I'm begging you. Could you do that somewhere else? I really need to be alone."

"Just pretend we're not here, honey," she said.

"I can do that with ninety-four percent of me," I answered. "But my nose part won't cooperate."

"Oh, does it smell bad in here?"

"I need goggles and a nose plug, Mom. No offense, Harry. I know you have to do what you have to do. I just wish you didn't have to do it in my room."

Wait a minute. What happens if that smell seeps into my dresser drawers and infiltrates my Mets sweatshirt? No amount of washing will return it to its wearable state.

"How long until Harry's potty trained, Mom? Not that I'm counting or anything."

"Oh, just another twenty months or so," my mom said. "Depending on how he takes to the potty."

There was no depending about it. I decided right then and there that I was going to duct tape the potty to his little behind until he got the hang of it. I mean, this was my room, too, and I didn't appreciate his fragrant contribution.

"You look upset, Hank, honey," my mom said. "Anything wrong?"

I threw myself on my bed, put my hands behind my head, and sighed deeply. It was the first time I had taken a breath of any kind since the clubhouse.

"Frankie and Ashley got into the smart kids middle school," I said. "And in case you didn't notice, I applied nowhere special."

My mom picked up Harry and carried him over to me. She sat down on the bed. Harry flashed me one of his crooked baby grins, and I couldn't resist asking my mom if I could hold him. She handed him to me, and he started sucking on my nose. Wow, he couldn't even tell his thumb from my nose. Obviously this kid wasn't destined for any brainiac school, either.

"We discussed your middle school path with Ms. Adolf," my mom said, looking squarely at me. "And she felt that your best and only option was to proceed to MS 245 with most of the other kids from your class."

"So you took Ms. Adolf's word for it?" I couldn't believe what I was hearing. "The only thing she's ever recommended me for is permanent detention."

"Honey, I know this is hard for you, but Frankie and Ashley are really excellent students. They belong in an accelerated program."

"And what about me?" I asked. "Where do I belong?"

"Okay, Hank," she said, taking Harry back from my arms. I guess she thought he had sucked on my nose long enough. She bounced him up and down on her knee as she spoke, and he giggled like a maniac. Sure, easy for him to giggle. He hasn't had any rejection yet in his life.

"Let's go through it, honey. What do we know? Well, we know that you're a great kid, very resourceful, full of energy, and well liked by everyone. But school is hard for you. That's just the fact."

There was that fact again. I hated that fact.

"So having you apply to an accelerated program wasn't the right decision. Even if you got in, it would be so difficult for you to keep up. You would constantly be under pressure, and your father and I didn't want you to have that kind of stress."

"Thanks a lot, Mom. But that still leaves me without my two best friends, which has never happened in my whole life. Why didn't you ask me what I wanted?"

"Because you're in the bottom three percent of all fifth-graders in the universe and beyond," came a voice. Don't worry, it wasn't my mother. She's nice and would never say anything like that, even if it was true.

It was Emily, of course, who can hardly wait to tell me how inferior I am to her in every way. Apparently, while my mom and Harry and I were talking, she and her pencil-neck boyfriend, Robert Upchurch, had slithered into my room, like the three-toed tree frogs they are.

"Emily, we're having a private discussion

here," my mom told her.

"As in make like a tree and leaf," I said.

"That's so funny, I forgot to laugh," Robert chimed in, as though he had just made up that phrase.

"Thank goodness, Robert, because every time you laugh, your nose starts to drip, and I wish you wouldn't do that on my carpet."

"Hank, you exaggerate so much," Emily said. "Robert's nose has never dripped on your carpet. The closest it ever came was that time on your desk."

"Eeuuwww," I said. "Were you guys in here when I wasn't?"

"It's not just your room, you know? It's Harry's room, too, and he said we could come in. He wanted to meet Robert."

I turned to Harry and said, "What were you thinking, little bro?"

"It was a scientific meeting," Robert said. "I'm studying the development of baby toes and fingers. See, I made this baby ruler out of construction paper. Did you know his little toe is exactly one-fourth of an inch long? I can convert that to centimeters if you'd like."

"Don't twist your brain into a tizzy, Robert. I can live without that piece of information."

"Well, let me tell you that your brother's toe is shorter than your mother's fingernail. Scientifically speaking, that is."

"Robert, could I ask you to leave now?" I said, trying to sound polite. "And take Emily with you?"

"We were just leaving, anyway," said Emily. "It's time to put Katherine down for her nap. Harry and Katherine are on the same schedule, you know?"

"I suppose you know that the iguana eyelid moves up from the bottom to cover the top eyelid when the animal is asleep," Robert added, as if anyone had been discussing iguana eyelids in the first place.

"I did know that, Robert. Oh, and here's something else I know. Wait. It's coming into my brain. Yes, here it is! It's time for you to leave."

Emily and Robert slithered out, just the same way they had slithered in. When I heard the door click behind them, I turned back to my mom.

"So, Mom. What am I going to do?"

"I'll tell you what we're going to do, honey.

Tomorrow morning, I'm going to call Principal Love and have a conference to discuss where you applied and which one will be the best middle school option for Hank Zipzer."

"I'd like to come to that conference," I said.

"I've never heard you say that before, Hank. And I agree with you. You should be there."

With that, Harry decided it was time for him to get in on the action. As I tickled him under his third chin, he laughed and belched at the same time. To me, it sounded like he was agreeing that I should be at the meeting.

Then he barfed up a little milk that landed on my jeans. I had no idea what that meant . . . except that it was time to change my jeans.

CHAPTER 8

The only good thing about the meeting with Principal Love was that I got to miss my math test. At eleven thirty, when Ms. Adolf told me it was time for me to leave class and join my parents in the school office, I jumped out of my chair, pumped my fist and shouted, "You don't have to tell me twice!"

"Henry," Ms. Adolf said. "Being called to the principal's is no cause for celebration, and absolutely no reason to be disruptive. I've told you over and over again, you are in great need of controlling your verbal outbursts."

"Come to think of it, Ms. Adolf, I was just having that very conversation with my lips and tongue."

The class cracked up. Ms. Adolf did not crack a smile, however. She didn't even crack a twitch. Instead, she tapped her gray shoe on the linoleum floor and folded her gray arms on her chest so that only her gray fingers were sticking out of her gray sleeves.

"When, and if, you advance to middle school, Henry, your childish antics will be appreciated even less."

"Is that even possible, Ms. Adolf?"

I didn't really mean to say that, either, but my lips and tongue had taken over my body.

"Zip it, Zip," Frankie whispered to me. "If you know what's good for you."

"I'm trying," I whispered back.

"Henry," Ms. Adolf said. "I suggest you remove yourself from my room before I am forced to give you even more detention than you have already."

I started to leave the room, with a bounce in my step and a tip in my toe, until I heard her parting words.

"It will be my pleasure to have your makeup math test waiting for you at lunch today."

Wow, couldn't that woman ever lighten up? I mean, I was on my way to the principal's office to discuss my entire future. That was no time to be thinking about decimal points.

As I walked downstairs to the office, I was suddenly struck with a bolt of panic. What if Ms. Adolf followed me to middle school like she did from fourth grade to fifth grade? Wait a minute. What if she follows me to high school? What if she's at my wedding? What if she's my bride? When the vision of her standing there in her gray wedding dress popped into my brain, I knew it was time to go to the water fountain and splash my face.

I was drying my face off with my shirt sleeve as I entered the outer office where Mrs. Crock, the school secretary, sits at her computer and usually has a plastic bowl of soggy salad. I checked out her desk. Yup, there it was. From the smell of it, I could tell it was her red onion day. Those were the days you liked to talk to her from a good distance if you wanted to stay out of her toxic breath zone. Once, when I got too close to her on red onion day, I walked into the office wearing a long-sleeved shirt and left with a short-sleeved shirt.

My parents were already sitting on the blue plastic chairs in the office, waiting for me. That was no surprise. They tend to be prompt for meetings in the principal's office.

But what was a surprise were the people Principal Love was escorting out of his office. None other than Nick the Tick McKelty and his dad. McKelty's dad must have made him comb his hair for the occasion. Instead of it looking like a rat's nest, it looked like he had used a can of axel grease to hold it down. With his hair slicked back, you could see his whole face, which took up most of the room. His cheeks were so large, you could play tennis on them.

"Hey, Zipperbutt," McKelty said under his breath. "What's a loser like you doing here?"

"Same thing as a loser like you," I whispered back to him.

"No way," he spit back.

I ducked to avoid a wad of saliva that flew out of his mouth. McKelty is a projectile speaker, which means you always have to watch very carefully because you never know what's going to come spewing out of his mouth when he talks. You can bet it's never going to be anything good, though, unless you happen to like getting six-month-old crusted mac 'n' cheese pellets plastered on your face.

"My dad and the principal just made a phone call about my future," he went on. "Looks like I'm going to a special studies program right inside the White House. The president himself is begging for me."

There it was. The McKelty Factor . . . truth times one hundred. Except this time, it was more like truth times a million.

"McKelty, if you go anywhere near the White House, they would arrest you for being the national creep you are."

"I know you are, but what am I?" he said.

"Nice comeback, as always," I said. "You certainly are on top of your game."

My dad, who noticed us talking, smiled and put a hand on my shoulder.

"It's nice to see you boys are such good friends," he said. "Our family has certainly enjoyed many hours of bowling at your family's bowling alley, Nick."

"Don't I know that!" Mr. McKelty said. "Randi, your dad still holds the record for the highest scorer in our senior league. He's just gotten a silver pass for a lifetime of free root beer."

That seemed to make my mom really happy.

I wondered how such a nice guy like Mr. McKelty could have produced such a mutant excuse for a son.

"I can see you in my office now," Principal Love said, turning to my parents. "And Mr. McKelty, thank you for coming in. I think Nicholas will really enjoy MS 245."

Oh, this was a great moment. I had Nick the Tick right where I wanted him.

"Nick!" I said, in a voice filled with surprise. "You had a choice between studying in the White House and MS 245 . . . and you chose to hang with us? Wow! I think I speak for the entire student body . . . we are so grateful!"

Mrs. Crock almost spit out her mouthful of leafy greens. My parents looked at each other, very confused. The Statue of Liberty mole on Principal Love's cheek started to twitch, getting ready to do the hula. Only Mr. McKelty could find the words to speak.

"Nick," he said, giving the Tick a harsh look, which was fun to see. "You haven't been making up outrageous stories again, have you?"

If I had a mouthful of leafy greens, I would have spit them out, too.

"No, Dad. I always tell the truth."

"Yeah," I said before my brain could stop my lips and tongue. "Truth times one hundred."

There it was. Finally out in the open.

"Nick's had a problem with that ever since he was little," his dad said.

It's a good thing I got control of my mouth area, because otherwise I would have said, "No kidding? Was he ever little?"

Mr. McKelty did not seem happy.

"Nick, we'd better get going," he said. "We don't want to keep the Zipzers from their meeting. Besides, you and I are going to have a little conversation about consequences."

"Dad, I don't know what you're talking about."

"You'll have plenty of opportunity to think about what I said while you're grounded in your room for the next two weeks."

That was music to my ears. No matter what was going to happen in Principal Love's office in the next few minutes, nothing could top that moment. It was one of the ten greatest sentences I could ever have heard.

CHAPTER 9

THE OTHER NINE GREATEST
SENTENCES I COULD EVER HAVE HEARD

1. Mr. Zipzer, your private roller coaster is ready for you now.
2. We're sorry to inform you that your sister, Emily, will have to repeat the fourth grade because she failed math, science, language arts, and she really sucked at spelling.
3. Ms. Adolf will no longer be teaching at PS 87 due to her decision to ride a barrel over Niagara Falls.
4. The Mets baseball organization is happy to inform you that you have been drafted and will start at first base in the World Series.
5. Hi, Hank, it's Katie Sperling. Would you like to see a movie Saturday afternoon . . . my treat?

6. I can't really focus on Number Six now because my head is still back with Katie Sperling, who is only the most beautiful girl in PS 87.

7. Okay, I'm better now.

8. Hi, Hank, it's Mom. I just bought a butt gadget which we can attach to Harry that will make his diapers smell like movie popcorn.

9. Your sister's iguana, Katherine, has just bought a plane ticket back to Brazil . . . one way.

10. Hank, your mother and I are so proud of you.

CHAPTER 10

Regular school (Robot Factory)

Ten minutes later, as we sat there listening to Principal Love drone on about my past, present, and future, I snuck a glance over at my dad and noticed that his left eye was starting to droop, which meant his right eye was not far behind. Principal Love has that effect on people—he's like a human sleeping pill. I watched my dad struggling to stay awake, and wanted to burst out laughing, but for one of the first times in my life, I actually exercised self-control.

Here, judge for yourself. This is what Principal Love was saying. See if you can stay awake.

"I believe that MS 245 is a fine choice for Hank, who is, as we've noted, a student with no particular outstanding educational characteristics. Of course, I think we can all agree that outstanding educational characteristics are rare, as characteristics go, and they include computing, compiling, synthesizing, constructing, deconstructing, and, of course, pasting. Good use of scissors and glue never hurts. In my own educational experience, I happened to excel at all fine motor skills, and I notice that those very same skills seem to provide Hank's fingers with an enormous challenge."

So this is a test, guys. Anyone still awake out there? If you are, you're a better, stronger person than my dad, who by now, had both eyes shut tight and was one second away from his chin smashing down on his chest. My mom had somehow managed to stay awake, and even got a word or two in.

"But surely, Principal Love," she said. "You have to agree that Hank has so many special qualities, also."

"Indeed I do agree, Mrs. Zipzer. Your son has a wonderful sense of humor . . . that he consistently uses at inappropriate times."

Wait a minute. Was that supposed to be a compliment, because it felt like someone had just kicked me hard in the shins.

My mom, bless her heart, went back in for another shot at the goal.

"We were hoping that there might be a special program for Hank in middle school that would make great use of all of his wonderful abilities."

"Mrs. Zipzer, you're not getting the big picture, so let me be even clearer. Hank, here, while a very energetic and popular comedian, is, academically speaking, a regular student. Now mind you, there is nothing wrong with regular. As a matter of fact, most regular people are regularly important to the functioning of our society as a whole. And a regular middle school like MS 245 is a perfect place for a regular person to train to be adequately regular. And I know for a fact, it has special classes for those students who are having trouble with their academics."

Boy, my shins were burning now . . . oh, in a *regular* kind of way, of course.

My dad startled awake. He must have dreamed that he had heard someone near him say the word regular at least fifty-five times. For a guy who loves crossword puzzles so much, his ears are very sensitive to words.

"So if I can paraphrase what you're saying," my dad chimed in. "You think Hank should go to this school?"

"I know he should, Mr. Zipzer."

So there it was. My fate was being decided by three people who forgot to ask me my opinion. Did anyone care that I don't consider myself regular? That even though I'm not a great student, I do learn things, just in my own time, in my own way. And you know what else? I'm interested in things. I like learning. I'd like to go to a special school where the teachers are really interested in helping me learn the best way I can. Did anyone take my imagination into account? Is there a school for kids who have an imagination filled with personality? Because if there is, I would get in for sure. And maybe even get straight As.

And while I was thinking all these thoughts, Principal Love was opening the door of his office and showing us out.

Where were we going? My mom was going to the Crunchy Pickle to make soylami sandwich platters. My dad was going home to stare at his computer screen.

And me, I was on my way to MS 245.

CHAPTER 11

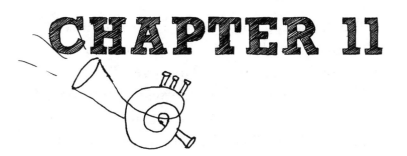

As if that meeting wasn't bad enough, I still had a makeup math quiz staring me in the face. And if *that* wasn't bad enough, I had to take it during my lunch period. And if *that* wasn't bad enough, I really studied for it and I still couldn't even figure out the first question. And if *that* wasn't bad enough, Luke Whitman, the class nose-picker, was taking a makeup test at the desk right next to mine and spent the whole time digging around in his left nostril. And if *that* wasn't bad enough, he tried to wipe his finger on my answer sheet.

By the end of school that day, I was ready not to ever go to middle school or any other school for that matter. But I had promised Mr. Rock that I would report to the music room every day for ten days, and I wasn't about to go back on that promise.

"Hey, Hank," he said as I strolled through the doorway of his class. "You don't look like your typical irrepressible Zipzer self."

"No, I'm not. And by the way, Mr. Rock, I have no idea what that word means."

He laughed. That felt good and already I noticed that the gray cloud above my head was starting to lift.

"Irrepressible, Hank, means that even if things get you down, you bounce back."

"Well, I'm not too bouncy right now."

"I have just the solution," he said, loosening his tie that I noticed had musical notes on it. "French horn polishing. It is an ancient remedy proven to cure the blues."

"Count me in," I told him. "My blues are so dark blue, they're navy."

Mr. Rock laughed again.

"You're funny, Hank. Everything you say is so original."

The gray cloud lifted even higher. It's amazing what a little appreciation from one human being can do for you.

Mr. Rock went to the instrument closet and came back carrying a beat-up, brown leather case. He opened it, and inside was a curvy large horn, sitting on a velvet cushion. The cushion looked great, but the horn, which was shaped like an oversized letter C, looked pretty beat-up. Not that I have much to compare it to, in the horn department. But it wasn't shiny and seemed to have a general layer of crud covering it.

"This French horn was returned today by one of your fellow fifth-graders," Mr. Rock said. "It needs a good cleaning, because for some strange reason, the inside is coated with food."

"Don't tell me," I said. "It was Nick McKelty's instrument."

"That's amazing, Hank! How'd you know that?"

"Because Nick McKelty is a food grinding machine. I swear, he's got parts of lunch in his mouth that are still there from the third grade."

Mr. Rock laughed again. I felt the gray cloud over my head drift up and away, through the ceiling, out the roof, and into the sky above the Upper West Side. Maybe it was going to make someone else feel bad, but not me. I was starting to feel like a brand-new guy.

"So what you're going to do is clean every

inch of this instrument with a soft cloth," Mr. Rock began.

"No problem," I nodded. "I can do that."

"Then you'll apply brass polish and rub out all the finger prints and scratches until the surface gleams."

"No problem. I can do that."

"Then you'll remove any collected saliva from the spit valve."

"We've just come across our first problem," I said. "This is Nick McKelty we're talking about. I cannot be in personal contact with his mouth liquid. I mean, there's a good possibility it will eat away my fingers and then I wouldn't be able to polish any more instruments, and I happen to know, you have a whole closet full of horns that need my attention."

By now, Mr. Rock was practically howling. But that didn't stop him from sitting me down at a table, handing me a soft cloth and a can of brass polish, and putting McKelty's cruddy French horn in front of me.

"You have your work cut out for you," he said, tossing me a pair of rubber gloves. "We only have an hour. I'm going to sit at my desk and enter my end-of-term grades. If you have any questions, ask me first before you take action. These are expensive instruments."

Mr. Rock went to his desk and started typing on his laptop computer. I picked up the horn in front of me. I didn't know where to start, but I certainly didn't want to start with the spit valve, so I turned my attention to the big opening.

"Wow, this probably makes a loud sound because the hole is so wide," I said.

Mr. Rock looked up from his desk and smiled.

"That part of the instrument is called the bell," he explained. "The French horn was actually developed from the hunting horns that European people used while hunting foxes."

"Poor foxes," I said. "The sound coming out of this baby would make your bones rattle."

As I started to polish the horn, I kept thinking about those foxes, running as fast as they could away from the fifty men and women chasing them on thundering horses. There was something about rubbing the brass over and over in a circular rhythm that allowed my brain to wander and I found myself thinking just like that fox . . . being chased.

"Wow, it's dangerous being a fox. Those guys on horseback are really on my tail. And the one in front, with the red coat and the white wig, he's got a gun. A gun! And he's aiming it at me! Legs, don't fail me now!"

Maybe my body was cleaning the bell of a French horn in the music room of PS 87, but my imagination was out in that field, being chased by those thundering horse hooves.

"I've got to find some cover. Good, there's an overgrown fallen tree at the bottom of that hill. If I can just make it there, I'll crawl under it and they'll never find me. Oh no, my leg's caught on this vine. Now what? Don't panic. Think. Okay, I'll chew through the vine. It's not that thick. Oh no, it's bitter. Yuck! Can't let that stop me now. I'll spit it out. Ptooey! All right, I can move my leg now. No time to see if it's bleeding. The horses are almost on top of me. Got to run. Got to run. Like the wind."

I hadn't actually intended to say all that out loud. But when I stopped for a second, I saw Mr. Rock staring at me. He wasn't touching his computer. He was just listening.

"I'm sorry, Mr. Rock," I said. "I didn't mean to be talking out loud, but sometimes my imagination gets carried away."

"That's one of your most unique qualities, Hank. Go on. I'm on the edge of my seat. What's the fox going to do next?"

I put the French horn down and stared at my reflection in the one shiny section I had already polished. Within a second, I wasn't looking at my face anymore. I was back in the body of the fox, running for my life.

"They're catching up to me. Maybe I can make it to Chagford Creek. If I run through the water, they won't be able to follow my scent. There's the creek, just ahead. Wow, I just caught a glimpse of my tongue. It's hanging out of my mouth, which means I really have to stop for a drink of water. No time for that now. Almost there. Just have to get through this thistle patch. Oooowww, my back. It's burning. I've been shot. I'm never making it to the creek, and I was so close. Good-bye, world. Good-bye, Barry Fox, my best friend. It's been swell. And good-bye, Mama Fox. I really love that gooseberry stew you used to make. And now, I die. WAIT A

MINUTE. I'm still running! I must not be dead. I just got poked by the thistles. I live. Now I'm wet. I'm swimming in the creek. And now the hounds are sniffing all over the place. They don't know which direction I've gone. I'm safe! I'm smart. I'm Hank!"

I looked up and Mr. Rock was standing at his desk, applauding wildly.

"Bravo," he shouted. "Well done, Hank!"

"It's nothing," I said. "When I'm in my room, my mind wanders and I make up these characters instead of doing my math homework. They just pop into my head to say hi. My dad says it's a loss of focus and lack of concentration."

"I know another word for it," Mr. Rock said.

I knew what was coming. I was waiting for any of those words everyone has always used to describe me. Lazy. Unfocused. Distracted. Underachieving. Take your pick.

"It's called talent," Mr. Rock said. "And you were born with it, Hank."

Talent? That was definitely not one of the words I was waiting for.

CHAPTER 12

The next day, I showed up in Mr. Rock's room actually on time and looking forward to the hour we would spend together. If you had told me two days before that I would enjoy staying after school to do community service, I would have said that your brain had turned into pea soup without the bacon. But just the chance to hang out with a teacher who thought that my imagination wasn't a nuisance was an incredible and totally new experience.

"Have a red vine," Mr. Rock said, pulling open the bottom drawer of his desk where he kept a humungous container of red licorice. "I find it perks up your afternoon."

"Thanks, Mr. Rock," I said as I chomped down on the top of the vine and pulled hard until it stretched to the breaking point and popped off in my mouth.

"Are you ready for the string section?" Mr. Rock asked.

"Sure. I'm into string. Are we flying kites or making a telephone out of two tin cans?"

"Neither, although those are both fun things to do. The strings I'm talking about refer to string instruments . . . which are instruments that are played with a bow."

"Hold it right there, Mr. Rock. Are you talking about a violin, because that has to be the worst instrument made by humans. My sister, Emily, took a lesson once in our apartment. The screech that came out of that thing shot into my ear and gave me goose bumps on my brain. It sounded like somebody being bitten by a vampire, not that I've ever been bitten by one."

Mr. Rock laughed and took a red vine for himself.

"Learning to play the violin can be tricky and painful for anyone who's listening. My older sister studied violin for years, and when she first began, our dog used to jump into the laundry basket and hide under my dad's shirts. Now she plays in the Cleveland Symphony Orchestra. That's what practicing anything can do for you,

Hank. You get better at it."

I thought about that for a minute. The good thing about Mr. Rock is that he says things that make you think. But my thinking time was interrupted by a familiar, thick voice calling me from the doorway.

"Hey, Zipperbutt," Nick McKelty shouted in. "I just wanted to see what a jerk doing community service after school looks like. And I was right. You look like a loser."

He held up his hand in the shape of an L and waved it in front of me. The only thing was he waved the wrong hand, so the L was backward. Even someone with dyslexia like me could see that.

"Thanks for the visit, Nick," Mr. Rock said. "And the next time you feel like visiting, I think you'll find it more constructive if you keep your negative thoughts to yourself."

"That's exactly what I'm going to do," the big lug said. Then, as he was leaving, he turned back and said, "By the way, I don't have that many negative thoughts."

"That's because you don't have any thoughts at all," I said, before I could stop myself.

"That goes for you, too, Hank," Mr. Rock whispered. "Don't stoop to his level."

Mr. Rock took me to the corner of the room where a whole bunch of leather cases were stacked up.

"There should be a violin and a bow inside each case," he said.

"Cool. Are there arrows in there, too?"

We both laughed. Mr. Rock really gets my humor.

"Different kind of bow," he said. "I'll bet you didn't know that a violin bow is made of horse-hair, specifically from the tail of a white male horse."

"Wow, I'm going to pull that fact out next time Robert Upchurch tries to show me up with one of his weird facts. Last night he told me that it's physically impossible for an astronaut to burp in space. Where does he come up with this stuff?"

"I need you to focus now, Hank. Back to business."

"Focusing as you speak, sir. Hank to brain, zero in."

Mr. Rock opened up a case and took out a violin and a bow.

"I want you to open these cases and record the number of each violin and each bow. You'll find the numbers on a white label somewhere on the instrument."

"Can do," I said.

Mr. Rock walked back to his desk, opened his briefcase, and pulled out a manila folder that was stuffed full of all kinds of papers—yellow pads, blue test booklets, white envelopes, pink post-its. It was so disorganized; it looked like a tornado hit it. He dumped all the papers out on top of his desk and started to put them in piles.

I picked up one of the violin cases and opened it. The violin and bow were tucked into their own purple velvet spaces. Without really thinking about what I was doing, I picked up the violin and tucked it under my chin. Then I picked up the bow to check out the horse tail hair. I held it to my ear to see if I could hear it whinny, but then I thought, *don't be silly, Hank. Tail hair doesn't whinny, even if it is on a horse.*

I took the violin from under my chin, held it in front of me and looked closely at it. What a weird shape it had, when you really studied it. It kind of looked like a little person, with the neck and the head and the curvy body. If it looked that weird to me, I wondered what it would look like to an alien from the planet Zork. Before I knew it, my brain was off and running . . . with my mouth running alongside.

"Hello, my little friend," I said to the violin. "I am Captain Lorch from the planet Zork. We come in peace. And speaking of peace, can I offer you a piece of our Zork candy? We call it Fudge-Ums. Here, pop one into your mouth. Oops, sorry you don't have a mouth. I don't suppose you'd want to pop one between your strings. Yes, I see. That could get very messy if it melted."

I heard Mr. Rock chuckle from his desk. I have to admit, I really liked hearing that. For me, having someone enjoy what I'm saying is like gas for a car . . . it makes me keep going. So I did.

"Did I tell you that you look so much like my brother Gorch? He also has pegs for ears and a long neck. However, he isn't made of wood, he's made of something you humans call beets. He's very red which comes in handy in his line of work. He's a night watchman who glows in the dark. And did I mention, it's dark twenty-four hours a day on Zork."

I was brought back to Earth from Zork when I saw two smiling faces standing in the doorway. It was Frankie and Ashley.

"Hey, Zip," Frankie said. "We thought we'd check in on you and see what's up."

"Yeah, we feel bad you're staying after school every day," Ashley added, "so we brought you some chocolate chip cookies we saved from lunch."

"I may look like Hank Zipzer to you, earthlings, but in fact, I am Captain Lorch from the planet Zork. I will accept your cookies in good fellowship as a symbol of intergalactic peace between our worlds."

Frankie and Ashley are used to me, so they just jumped right in without blinking an eye.

"Captain Lorch," Frankie said. "How will you eat these cookies? Are they not a strange foodstuff to you?"

"Not after you've eaten some of the goop my mother makes."

Ashley and Frankie cracked up so hard, I thought they couldn't catch their breath. It must have been contagious, because Mr. Rock started to laugh really hard, too.

I walked over to Ashley, doing my funny alien walk which I sometimes practice in my room in front of my mirror instead of doing multiplication tables. I reached out, took the cookies and the plastic bag they were in, and stuffed them in my mouth.

"Your earth cookies look like chocolate, but have no taste."

"On our planet, we think it's more enjoyable if you unwrap the cookies first," Ashley said, her eyes watering like she was crying, only the tears came from laughing.

"On Zork, we eat through our bellybuttons," I said. "I will demonstrate."

I held the cookies over my bellybutton and tugged on my earlobe.

"This is the on switch that starts the process," I said. Then I made a noise like a vacuum cleaner and spun around three times, stuffing the cookies in my jeans pocket as I was spinning. When I came to a stop, I said, "Those discs with chocolate specs were delicious. We have nothing like that on Zork. They would be excellent with a glass of milkum."

I could hardly finish the sentence because Frankie and Ashley and I were all laughing so hard. Before I knew it, I felt Mr. Rock's hand on my shoulder.

"We have to talk about this, Hank," he said.

"I'm sorry, Mr. Rock," I said, trying to get control of myself. "I guess I got too carried away."

"He does that a lot," Frankie said. "Once his imagination gets going, it takes off like a rocket."

"Yeah," Ashley agreed. "Hank is the king of getting carried away. Don't get mad at him. He can't help it."

"I'm not angry at all," Mr. Rock said. "What I am is amazed. I've always known you are clever and verbal and funny, Hank. But what I've watched you do over the last two days shows me that you have a unique gift. Your ability to create characters and voices and to improvise . . . it's quite extraordinary."

"Something tells me I'd appreciate what you're saying a whole lot more, Mr. Rock, if I knew what improvise meant."

"When you improvise, it means you make

something up on the spot. You reach inside yourself and pull out a performance without a script or written music. It's what the great jazz musicians do."

"Like my dad's favorite trumpet player, Miles Davis," Frankie chimed in.

"Your dad has good taste," Mr. Rock said.

"I don't think I could be a trumpet player," I said, shaking my head. "I'm supposed to get braces next year, and it would really hurt my lips to press the trumpet up against my braces, metal to metal."

"Hank, I want you to come with me right away," Mr. Rock said. "Frankie and Ashley, will you excuse us, please? Hank and I have something very important to do."

Mr. Rock was almost out the door before he had finished the sentence. I grabbed my backpack, shrugged my shoulders and followed him. He was in a big hurry to take me someplace.

I wished I knew where.

CHAPTER 13

Mr. Rock was practically running down the hall, and I had to really hustle to keep up.

"Slow down, Mr. Rock. There's no running in the hall."

"If we were ever going to break the rules, Hank, this is the perfect occasion," he yelled over his shoulder. "We're on a mission—Project Hank. We're about to launch you into your future."

"I wish I had worn my space helmet."

Mr. Rock was in such a hurry, he didn't even stop to laugh. We raced down the stairs and across the hall to the counselor's office where I meet with Dr. Lynn Berger once a week. On the glass window in the door there was a sign that said, "If it's urgent, you can find me in the gym."

Without even stopping to catch his breath, Mr. Rock was off again, climbing up the stairwell to the gym, taking two steps at a time. Another rule broken. Wow, it's a good thing I was with a teacher, because if it had been during school and one of the hall monitors caught me running like that, I'd be in detention for nine months.

As we approached the gym, I could hear music blaring through the double doors. It was a rock-and-roll song I'd never heard before, but it sounded like the weird disco stuff my parents dance to every year on their anniversary. Boy, you haven't lived until you've seen Stanley Zipzer doing his special step. It looks like he's actually mashing potatoes with his feet. And funnily enough, the step is called the Mashed Potato. I tell you, adults are weird.

Mr. Rock opened the gym door, and what I saw made my eyes spin backward in my head. There they all were in front of me—Mrs. Crock, Dr. Berger, Principal Love, Mr. Sicilian, and Ms. Adolf, wearing different exercise outfits and dancing, if you want to call it that, to the music. They were all hooting and hollering and waving their arms up in the air.

"Mr. Rock, what exactly are they doing?" I

asked. "Are they rehearsing for a play, because if they are, they should stop selling tickets right away."

"It's the faculty and staff exercise class," Mr. Rock whispered back to me. "They work out three times a week after school."

"Oh," I nodded. "They're working out. Is that what you call it?"

"Wait here. I'm going in to get Dr. Berger."

As I stood there at the door watching the workout session, I noticed that poor Principal Love was trying his hardest to keep up with everybody else. His mind said yes, but his legs said no. Even the Statue of Liberty mole on his cheek was moving a lot smoother than he was. He was wearing his gee, the outfit which he uses to teach Tae Kwon Do after school. The only problem was that the legs and arms were too short for him, so he looked like a turtle wearing a marshmallow. Trust me, it wasn't pretty.

And speaking of not pretty, you should have seen Ms. Adolf. She was wearing a gray leotard and gray tennis shoes and whooping like a crane. I don't mean a baby crane. She was whooping like it was the last whoop left in the universe. She must have had too much candy before they started, because she looked like she was on what my mom calls a sugar high. I tried to hide behind the door, but her eyes caught me before I was out of sight.

"Come exercise, Henry," she called. "It stimulates your nerve endings which in turn might improve your spelling."

I slid down the door onto the floor. Can you imagine me, dancercising with Ms. Adolf, having to duck most of the time to avoid being splashed by her gray sweat? I'm sorry I said that. I now have to find some soap and wash that thought out of my brain.

Thank goodness for Mr. Rock. He came out into the hall with Dr. Berger following right behind him. She was out of breath, and dabbing her forehead with her dancercise towel.

"Yes, gentlemen," she panted. "What is so important that it can't wait until I'm finished?"

"Hank's future, that's what," Mr. Rock said.

Dr. Berger raised her eyebrows. "That got my attention," she said.

"For the last several days," Mr. Rock began,

"I've had the opportunity to witness firsthand Hank's extraordinary talent at portraying characters and creating situations that he makes up on the spot and performs flawlessly."

"Really? You did?" I asked. "Is that what I was doing?"

"This young man has real talent and I don't think sending him to a school without a theater arts program would benefit him. There's got to be another alternative."

"Well, there is the Professional Performing Arts School," Dr. Berger answered.

I'd heard of that school before. My cousin Amanda went there, but she was a really talented ballet dancer. I think my mom said she's with the big deal ballet company of Paris. Or maybe Shanghai. Or maybe Denver. It's one of those, I can't remember.

"Wow. That school's for super-talented kids. Would they take me?"

"You'd have to audition, Hank," Dr. Berger explained. "So they can see your talent."

My heart started to beat fast. The possibility of going to that school was really exciting. I mean, wow.

"Great," Mr. Rock said. "Let's try to set up the audition."

"Unfortunately, the audition process ended several months ago," Dr. Berger said. "I believe it's much too late."

I knew it was too good to be true.

"However," Dr. Berger said, putting her hand on my shoulder. "I'm very willing to make a phone call to find out if they make exceptions."

"Great," I said. "You don't happen to have your cell phone on you, do you?"

"I don't usually exercise with it," she answered. "I'll make the call tomorrow, Hank."

I didn't say a word, just kept staring at her. Then Dr. Berger looked through the open door to the gym and saw that Ms. Adolf was leading the class in an enthusiastic version of a disco favorite. She smiled at me.

"The class is in good hands," she said. "Let's go to my office and use the phone there."

As we walked down the stairs to Dr. Berger's office, my mind was swimming with thoughts. Ten of them, to be exact.

CHAPTER 14

**TEN THOUGHTS THAT WERE
SCREAMING IN MY MIND ON THE WAY
TO DR. BERGER'S OFFICE**

1. Let them say yes.
2. Let them say yes.
3. Let them say yes.
4. Let them say yes.
5. Let them say yes.
6. Let them say yes.
7. Let them say yes.
8. Let them say yes.
9. Let them say yes.
10. Let them say yes.

CHAPTER 15

They did ſay yeſ.

As it turned out, the regular auditions were over, but there was a makeup day, and it was scheduled for the next Saturday. At first they said I couldn't audition because it was too late, but Dr. Berger told them that they really should meet me, which made me feel great. But then they said that the other reason I couldn't audition was that I hadn't filled out the application for the school. But when Dr. Berger assured them that I would do the application that night and have my parents drop it by in the morning, they said yes.

Wow, they said yes!

CHAPTER 16

Mr. Rock walked me home so that he could explain the situation to my parents, and help me fill out the application. I carried the manila folder with the application that the school had faxed to Dr. Berger's office. Knowing how things seem to disappear in my backpack and never return, I was afraid to put it in there. I didn't want to take any chances that it would wind up covered in sticky gum wads like my community service notice.

"How do you think your parents are going to feel about you applying to the Professional Performing Arts School?" Mr. Rock asked as we crossed Amsterdam Avenue.

"Well, my mom is pretty strong in the supportive department. My dad, on the other hand, will probably stare at me for forty-five seconds and then give me one of his crossword puzzle answers . . . two letters across, two letters down, both of them N and O."

"Hey, Hank, you have to think positively. Why would you think your dad would immediately say no?"

We were walking past Mr. Kim's grocery store now, and I waved to him as he was organizing the orange display.

"Because it's his favorite word in the English language. Remember when you came to our house to tell my parents you thought I had a learning challenge? What was the first thing my dad said to you? Let me refresh your memory," I went on, before Mr. Rock could even respond. "He said, 'NO, he doesn't.'"

"You have a point there," Mr. Rock agreed. "But maybe this time it will be different."

By then, we had reached the front door to my apartment building. I used my key to get into the lobby, and then pushed the button for the elevator. While we were waiting for it to come, I noticed that my foot seemed to be tapping like it had a mind of its own. I tried to make it stop by stepping on it with my other foot, but all that did was make me say, "Ouch." I think my foot was telling me that I was nervous.

It was not the only part of my body talking to me. By the time we got into the elevator, my stomach had joined in, flipping around like an acrobat in the circus. I really wanted this audition to happen, but it wasn't up to me. My foot and my stomach were shouting to Stanley Zipzer, "Let the kid give it a try. Maybe he'll get into this school." But I knew from experience that Stanley Zipzer was a tough nut to crack.

Mr. Rock wasn't prepared for what he saw when I opened the door to our apartment. Katherine, who is usually the laziest iguana in captivity, was running down the linoleum hallway at a speed I had no idea was in her. On her tail, and I mean actually on her tail, was our dachshund, Cheerio, chasing her like she was his favorite biscuit with legs. Usually, Cheerio gives Katherine a lot of space and pretty much ignores her. But she must have thrown one too many hissy fits in his direction, and the poor guy finally cracked. He was barking and growling and yipping all at the same time.

Right behind Cheerio was Emily, shrieking at the top of her lungs.

"Bad dog, Cheerio!" she hollered. "Katherine didn't mean to hiss at you. She was just trying to tell you that you were invading her personal space."

But Katherine and Cheerio kept running. You could tell even if you weren't looking at her, because you could hear her iguana nails and his wiener doggy nails clicking along the linoleum.

"Here, Cheerio," my mom called out, coming into the hall from the kitchen. "Leave Katherine alone and come get a treat Mommy baked for you. It's a yummy wheatgrass and Brazil nut doggy biscuit."

Cheerio stopped in his tracks and gave my mom's biscuit a sniff. Instead of taking a bite, he started to sneeze. And not just one sneeze, but a whole slew of them.

"Bless you, honey," my mom said. "Now take a bite."

Cheerio looked at my mom's face as if to say, "Wheatgrass and Brazil nuts . . . are you kidding?"

Then he turned on his short but swift back two legs and took off after Katherine, who by this time, had bolted into the living room and was trying to dig a hole through the rug.

"I've found the net," my dad hollered, running out of his bedroom waving an old trout fishing net that he kept by his desk and used for nerf basketball practice.

"No, Dad!" Emily screamed. "You can't trap Katherine in that net. It's disgusting. It smells like old fish."

But there was no talking to my dad, who was already crawling around the living room on his knees, trying to swoop Katherine up in the net.

"Welcome to the Zipzer looney farm," I whispered to Mr. Rock.

"Seems like a regular family to me," he said with a smile.

Thank goodness Papa Pete was there or my family would still be running around the apartment like they were caught in a never-ending fire drill.

"Here, Cheerio," he said, coming out of the kitchen, and holding a real world treat in his hand. "I got a nice slice of corned beef for you."

Cheerio didn't even stop. He just spun in a circle and made a beeline for Papa Pete. Well, actually not for Papa Pete, but for his corned beef.

He gobbled that meat down without even taking the time to chew, and his tail started to wag so fast, I could feel the wind against my cheek. Cheerio's corned beef break gave Katherine the opportunity to jump into Emily's arms and bury her head in her armpit. I'm surprised that stupid reptile didn't pass out from the fumes.

Emily immediately ran into her room, and put Katherine back into her glass tank.

"I'm going to play Kathy some classical music," she said, "to soothe her nerves. Tell me, Kathy. Do you want Beethoven or Mozart?"

"Like that lower life-form knows the difference," I yelled at her.

Emily slammed the door shut with her foot, which is her favorite comeback to one of my jokes.

It was at that moment that all the adults in the room finally looked up and noticed that Mr. Rock was in the apartment. My mom turned beet red, like one of her vegetable concoctions, and started to stammer.

"Oh my. This is so embarrassing. I didn't notice you were here. You must think we're . . . oh my. Well, hello. Hi. I mean hi there. I mean hi there, Mr. Rock."

"Mom, you just said hello eight times," I pointed out.

"Won't you come in?" she said to Mr. Rock. "Come into the living room and have a seat."

My mom gestured to the couch, and Mr. Rock took a seat. But no sooner had his butt hit the cushion, than he was standing up again. He reached down and picked up a green plastic rattle shaped like a dragon that belonged to my baby brother, Harry.

"I think this belongs to the youngest Zipzer," Mr. Rock said, handing my mom the rattle.

"I've been looking for that," my mom said, turning beet red for the second time.

All the grown-ups sat down and there was a moment of tense silence. I could tell my dad was preparing himself for bad news. I mean, when a teacher shows up at your house, it usually is a total disaster.

"Hank," Mr. Rock said, finally. "Why don't you show your parents what you have in the manila folder that you're holding?"

"Let me just prepare myself," my dad said. "Is this another notification of failure?"

"Stanley," my mom said, a little embarrassed at my dad's gruff tone. "Let Hank explain what he's got before we jump to conclusions."

I looked down at the application and took a deep breath. As I passed the folder to my dad, I noticed that my hands were trembling. Then I snuck a glance at my dad's face as he opened the folder and looked at the first page. His face instantly transformed into the face I saw when I was four and broke all the lead points on his new set of mechanical pencils.

Let me just say, this was not a happy man.

CHAPTER 17

My dad looked over the papers in the manila folder for forty-five seconds, sat back, moved his glasses from his nose to up on top of his forehead, and said his most favorite word in the English language.

You guessed it. NO.

"No what?" I said. "I didn't even ask anything."

"No on everything," my dad said. "All of it."

"Just like that? Without an example? My teacher always says you have to give examples to support your arguments."

"All righty, then," my dad said. "No, because this Performing Arts whatever it is, is not a normal school with a normal education that you can use for the rest of your life. And no because performing is too hard, nobody makes a living at it. And no, because it's not what we Zipzers do. We don't perform like circus cats. We work for a living . . . a concept you will become well acquainted with as you get older."

My dad sat back in his chair, satisfied with his explanation.

"But, Dad," I said, "that's only three measly examples."

"Well, try this one on," he said without missing a beat. "There has never been a Zipzer in show business or on the stage. It's all superficial."

My mom took my dad's hand and gave him a little squeeze. She does that when she's trying to soften him up or calm him down.

"Stanley, don't you remember your grandmother's cousin Alfred? She told me once that Alfred taught the great magician Houdini to swim, so he could do his underwater escape trick in the Hudson River."

My father looked annoyed. He wasn't at all happy with my mother uncovering a performing Zipzer. But me, I was thrilled.

"Wow!" I said. "I never knew that. Now I know where I got my talent as a magician. I can't wait to tell Frankie."

Mr. Rock had been sitting quietly, listening to our conversation, if you want to call it a conversation. It was more of a lecture, which by the way, it often is when you're talking to my dad. He talks. You listen. Subject closed. Anyway, Mr. Rock cleared his throat and asked if it would be all right if he expressed his opinion. My dad didn't answer, but my mom told him we would all be very interested in his opinion.

"Over the years, I have spent a great deal of time with your son," he began, "and it's my opinion that Hank has a gift that I believe needs to be nurtured. We all know how difficult school is for Hank. But when he is allowed to use his imagination, his intelligence comes shining through."

"We see that all the time," my mom said. "Hank entertains us at the dinner table and makes us all laugh. Isn't that right, Stanley?"

"You're missing the point, Randi. You can't feed a family by making them laugh or telling a cute story here and there. Hank needs a formal education."

"I couldn't agree with you more, Mr. Zipzer," Mr. Rock said. "And let me assure you that there is a very good formal education which is part of the curriculum at Professional Performing Arts."

"Let me just try out for this school, Dad," I said. "Please. I probably won't get in, anyway." I was thinking as fast as I could here. "And auditioning will be a great *educational* experience. You have to admit that."

My father just sat on the couch, scratching his chin. I was so involved in making my case that I hadn't noticed Emily standing at the entrance to the living room, Katherine draped around her neck. I guess they had finished their Mozart moment and Katherine was calm enough to be around humans again. I can't necessarily say the same for Emily, but there she was, anyway.

"Could I say something about this?" Emily asked.

I wanted to say no. I mean, the last thing I needed was brainchild Emily putting me down. When it comes to me, she always takes my dad's side.

"Kathy and I share a strong opinion about Hank's future," she said.

"Oh great," I said. "Now my future is in the claws of an iguana."

Emily shot me a look that said, "Keep your mouth shut for once, will you?"

"Daddy," she said. "We think that Hank is one of the funniest people on Earth. Annoying, but funny."

My ears started to twirl around on my head. Were they really hearing this? Nice words from my sister Emily? Not possible. But she wasn't finished.

"Like take me," she went on. "I happen to be excellent at science. It's a well-known fact in the fourth-grade science club that I am the expert on reptiles and small-boned rodents. So when I go to middle school, for sure I'm going to try to get into a gifted and talented science program. But Hank is gifted, too. Just different. And he should have the chance to shine, too, just like I do."

I couldn't believe what I said next. I didn't plan it, but the words just flew out of my mouth.

"Thanks, Em," I said. "I'm lucky to have you as a sister."

"You kids," my mom said, her eyes getting shiny like they do just before she's going to cry. "I love you both."

She popped up from her chair and attempted

to give Emily a hug, but Katherine threw a big-time hiss in her direction, so I got the hug instead. Then she turned to my dad, who was twirling the tip of his red mechanical pencil, making the lead go in and out. That was a good sign, because he does that mechanical pencil thing when he's thinking.

"We're raising good kids, Stanley," my mom said to him. "Emily made a really good point. How about if we let Hank audition? Then we'll see what happens."

The pencil lead went in and out. I started counting how many times. One, two, three, four, five, six, seven. Just before eight, he said yes.

CHAPTER 18

Mr. Rock and I got busy preparing for the audition. We met every day after school in the music room, and this time, there was no instrument cleaning involved. He would throw out subjects, and I would make up monologues. One day he told me to be a bottle of mustard being squirted on a hot dog. Another day he told me to be a baby kangaroo that fell out of his mom's pouch. He encouraged me to let my mind be free and to say whatever came to me.

If I made a mistake or couldn't think of anything, I felt embarrassed, but he explained that if you stumble, you have to stand right back up and keep moving forward. He said that one of the secrets of good acting is trial and error, which means that you only learn by making mistakes. Boy, try telling that to Ms. Adolf. To her, making a mistake is like the end of the world.

She's got that red pencil sharpened and ready to write the word FAIL at the drop of a hat.

We practiced every day that week, and by the time Friday came, I had told about a thousand stories. I was as ready as I was ever going to be, except for one thing. I was nervous about the audition. And not just your garden variety nervous. This kind of nervous started at my toes and ended up at my hair roots.

"What's with you, man?" Frankie asked as we walked home from school on Friday. "You've called me Theodore three times today. What's up with that?"

"I guess this audition tomorrow has taken up most of my brain. I don't have room for names anymore."

"I have a great idea," Ashley said. "You could use some relaxation before tomorrow. Frankie and I are taking you bowling this evening."

"We are?" Frankie said.

"Yes, we are." Ashley stopped for a minute and looked in the window of the drug store on the corner. I saw her glancing at an American flag pin that was made up of red, silver, and blue rhinestones. "Look at all those rhinestones," she said. "I could make a whole school of dolphins on my sneakers with those."

"I thought we were talking about bowling here, Ashweena," Frankie said. "How'd rhinestones come up?"

"Rhinestones, Frankie, are a great addition to any conversation," Ashley answered.

Frankie and I gave each other a look. The one thing you can't do with Ashley is insult her rhinestoning ability, which is actually pretty artistic.

"I think bowling sounds like a great idea," I said. "I'll call Papa Pete as soon as I get upstairs. I bet he would love to take us to McKelty's."

When I called and asked him, Papa Pete was in seventh heaven. The only thing he loves more than bowling is us kids, and when you put the two of them together, the guy is happier than a bug in a rug.

After dinner, he picked us up at my apartment. Before we left, I saw him open the refrigerator and put a plastic container inside.

"What's that?" I asked him.

"You'll see, Hankie. First things first."

We met Ashley and Frankie down in the

lobby and all walked up Amsterdam Avenue to McKelty's Roll 'N' Bowl. When we pushed open the leather doors and went inside, the first sound we heard was the clatter of bowling balls rolling down the lanes and striking the pins. The second thing we heard was everybody calling out hello to Papa Pete. He's a regular at McKelty's, and as a matter of fact, there's a new picture of him over the shoe checkout desk because two weeks before, he scored another perfect three hundred. What a bowler.

Papa Pete got us all fitted in shoes and picked his favorite lane, which is number seven. He always says that seven is his favorite number because he got married to my grandma Jenny on the seventh day of the seventh month in 1947.

I tried to concentrate on my bowling, but my mind kept drifting back to the audition. Papa Pete could tell something was wrong immediately because I rolled four gutter balls in a row.

"Somebody doesn't have his head in the game," he said. "Come on, Hankie. What did I teach you?"

"Zip's been out of it all day," Frankie said. "The guy's like a space cadet."

"Come on, Frankie," Ashley said. "Give him a break. He's got a big audition tomorrow. You know what, Hank? I have an idea on how to get your mind off it. Don't try to get your mind off it."

"Is it just me," I asked, "or did you just say something really confusing?"

"It's what I do," Ashley explained. "When I can't stop thinking about something, I don't try. I just go with it."

"Once again, young lady," Papa Pete said to her, "you show great wisdom."

"Okay," I said. "I'm going to take that wisdom and roll with it. Watch this."

I picked up a bowling ball with orange swirls on it. I'm a little embarrassed to say that because it's the kind that little kids use, but the truth is, it's lighter and that makes it easier for me to aim.

"I am a bowling ball," I said. "I know . . . you've noticed. But did you know that it's hard to be taken seriously when you're all orange and swirly. People think you're squishy, like an overripe cantaloupe, that you can't smack those pins like the typical black ball. It's lonely being orange."

Ashley and Frankie were laughing like maniacs. Papa Pete had a smile under his bushy mustache that lit up his entire face.

"Throw the ball, Hankie," he said. "I'm going to get you guys root beer floats."

After Papa Pete left, I took aim and let the ball fly off my fingers, but I carried on as though I was still the ball.

"Ouch, I'm getting wood burn from rolling down this lane. I guess they didn't put down enough oil. Uh-oh. There's the gutter. I'm not going there. I'm leaning to the left. Oh no, too far to the left. Here comes the other gutter. I'm leaning to the right, straight at the center pin. Here I come, buddy. You're mine."

When the orange ball struck, it actually clipped the very edge of one pin, which teetered for a long minute and finally fell backward, leaving the other nine standing at attention.

"Aaarrrgggfff," I grunted, in my best impression of a bowling ball crashing into the back of the lane. "That hurt. Anyone have a ball Band-Aid?"

I turned around, expecting to receive a round of applause from Frankie and Ashley, but standing right in front of them was the mouth breather of all time, Nick the Tick McKelty.

"A ball Band-Aid?" he said. "Are you serious? They don't make those."

"Thanks for the tip, McKelty. I wouldn't have known that without you."

"Listen, Zipperbutt. Maybe if you shut up when you're rolling, you could hit more than one pin," he said. "Nobody talks when they bowl."

"For your information, Nick," I shot back, "that wasn't me talking. That was the bowling ball."

"Bowling balls do not talk," he said. "And I should know because my dad owns fifty bowling alleys around the world. In fact, he's in Antarctica right now, buying two more igloo bowling alleys for penguins."

A tall, blond kid named Anderson Negley, who I knew from my old Little League team, was bowling on the lane next to us. He stopped mid-throw and looked over at McKelty.

"You expect any of us to believe that?" he said. "Everyone knows your dad owns one bowling alley and this is it. Besides, moron, have you ever seen a penguin bowl?"

"Have you ever seen one NOT bowl?" McKelty shot back.

"That makes so little sense, I can't even answer it," Anderson said. Then he turned to me. "Your name is Hank, right?"

"Yeah. I've seen you in Dr. Berger's office."

"Right. I think you had the appointment after mine. Listen, man, you being the ball was funny stuff. Cracked me up."

"Hank's rehearsing for an audition tomorrow," Ashley said. Then she gave him a really deluxe smile.

Where did that smile come from? I'd never seen it before. Wait a minute. Ashley was flirting with this guy. Whoa. I guess that's what girls do. But I never thought of Ashweena as a girl before.

"An audition?" McKelty snorted. "The only thing Zipperhead would get into is the city zoo. And that's already a stretch."

"McKelty, you're going to have to eat those words after Hank gets into the Professional Performing Arts School," Frankie said.

"That school?" McKelty said. "I wouldn't go to that loser school if you paid me."

"Listen, dude," Anderson chimed in. "I don't think you have to worry about that. No one is paying you to go anywhere."

"I'm paying him," came a voice from behind us. It was Nick's dad, delivering the three root beer floats that Papa Pete had ordered. "Nick, I thought I asked you to spray the shoes with disinfectant. That's what I'm paying you for, not to stand around and disturb the customers."

"But . . . Dad," McKelty tried to answer.

"No buts," his dad said sternly. "Just spray."

McKelty shuffled his big butt back to the shoe counter. As I watched him pick up the can of disinfectant and begin to spray the inside of a bunch of stinky shoes, I thought sometimes people get exactly what they deserve.

I really hoped that the next day, I would get just what I deserved, too . . . a place at Professional Performing Arts.

CHAPTER 19

After bowling, Papa Pete walked us home. It was one of those New York spring evenings that are just perfect, the kind that say winter is over and summer is on the way. As we walked down Amsterdam Avenue, passing the dry cleaners, the library, and the pet store where I bought Rosa, my pet tarantula, I kept taking deep breaths to calm myself down. The places we were passing, usually so familiar, were all a blur to me now. I realized that the audition was getting closer and closer, with every step we took. That's all I could think about.

When we got to our building, we rode up in the elevator and stopped at Frankie's floor first. Before he got out, he turned to me and looked me square in the eye.

"I'd wish you good luck tomorrow, Zip, but you don't need it. You'll knock 'em dead."

Then we bumped our fists, our elbows, and our butts. Nothing more needed to be said.

Next we stopped at Ashley's floor to let her off. She just threw her arms around me and gave me a gigantoid hug.

"I demand that you call me the minute you're out of the audition," she said. "I'm going to go to sleep tonight with my fingers crossed."

"Ow," I said. "That sounds painful."

She laughed and gave me one more hug before leaving the elevator.

Papa Pete and I got out on the tenth floor without saying a word. In our apartment, my dad was watching TV with Emily, some show about the Great Flu Epidemic of 1911. Boy, that's what I call a happy hour. My mom was putting Harry to bed in MY room, which as far as I can see, is how he spends ninety percent of his time. The other ten percent is spent eating, burping, and pooping. And let me tell you, I am completely aware of his poop time. My room has become the Kingdom of Poopdom.

"Meet me on the terrace in two minutes," Papa Pete said to me. "You and I have a hot date with a pickle."

I pushed open the door in the living room that leads out to the terrace. The stars were out, and if I looked one way, I could see the Hudson River. If I looked the other way, I saw the Museum of Natural History. There were lights on in all the apartments, as far as my eyes could see. All those people at home, relaxing and enjoying the evening. I wondered if there was anyone in any of those apartments who was as nervous as I was at that very moment.

Papa Pete tapped me on the shoulder and I jumped about fifty feet in the air.

"Wow," Papa Pete said. "Somebody's edgy. Relax, Hankie. It's just me bringing your pickle."

He reached into a plastic bag, and took out two thick cucumber-shaped pickles, handed one to me, and took the other one for himself.

"These are new pickles," Papa Pete said. "Nice and crunchy."

In case you're not a pickle expert like Papa Pete and I, let me explain that new pickles are taken out of the pickling juice and spices before they're totally done. That makes them taste sort of like a cucumber, but with a tang. Put one of those babies with a corned beef sandwich, and you are in delicatessen heaven.

We each pulled up a chair and took a bite of our pickles. There was a lot of crunching going on. Finally, Papa Pete turned to me and said, "So, Hankie, big day tomorrow, huh?"

"Funny you should bring that up," I said to him. "I was thinking of making it a medium day and calling the school and telling them that I can't make the audition."

"Really? And what would keep you from showing up at such an important event in your life?"

"Well, Papa Pete, I have a lot to do. For one, I promised Mom that I would organize my closet, and she's really counting on me to do that. I have to set a good example for Baby Harry. Which reminds me, I also have to teach Baby Harry to play toe basketball, and there's no time like tomorrow to begin. You can't start too early with these kids."

"Ahhh," Papa Pete said. "I think I'm hearing someone who's very nervous."

"I'm not nervous," I protested. "Really. It's just that I have a lot of stuff to get done and that audition doesn't fit in with my schedule. So I'll do it another time. Like next year. Or the year after. Or the year after that."

Papa Pete took another bite of his pickle and just sat there enjoying the taste before he said anything else. Then he put his big hand on my shoulder and gave it a squeeze.

"Hankie," he said. "You don't need me to lecture you, but just take a moment and look deep down inside, way into your guts."

"I'm doing it, Papa Pete. And all I'm seeing is chewed pickle."

Papa Pete laughed. I love it when he laughs because it starts at his toes and by the time it comes out of his mouth, it's really loud and joyous.

"I think along with that pickle you'd see a boy who wants something very badly and has a really good chance at getting it, but is too afraid to try. You have your future in your hands, Hankie, but you have to take action to make it happen."

"But how do you know I'm any good? Maybe Dad is right! Maybe we Zipzers don't do this performance thing!"

"I say this not because you are my grandson, but because I have observed you for a long time. You are a very talented young man. And you can take that to the bank."

"What if I stink tomorrow? What if I just stand there and freeze up like a popsicle? I don't want to take a chance on that."

"You're not the only one who has these feelings," Papa Pete said. "All successful people are afraid to take chances, just like you are now. But most of them don't allow that to stop them from reaching for the stars."

"See, there you go," I said. "Problem solved. I'm too short to reach for the stars. So I'm staying home. Thanks, Papa Pete, for helping me figure that out."

"Hankie," he said, looking me right in the eye. "I can promise you this. The one thing worse than feeling afraid of failure is the feeling that you never tried. If you don't try, you'll never know."

I didn't have a funny answer for that one. There was a serious tone in Papa Pete's voice that told me I'd better listen to what was coming next.

"I remember when I was a young man," he began, clearing this throat, "and had a dream to start my own restaurant. My father wanted me to go into his lumber business, buying and selling wood from all over the world. But I wasn't interested in wood at all. Sure, I liked a chair to sit on as well as the next guy. But that's as far as my interest in wood went."

Papa Pete stood up and looked out onto the lights of New York. I could tell he was remembering every detail from a long time ago.

"But my father was a strong man, and I was afraid to go against him. So I went into the wood business. For ten years, I bought and sold wood. And I never ever enjoyed it. Not for a minute. Then I met your grandma Jenny. She gave me the best advice ever."

"What was it?" I asked, standing up to be next to him.

"It was just what I'm telling you now. That if you don't try to make your dreams come true, you'll never know. So, Hankie, my boy, you have to overcome whatever fear you have at this moment, and give it a shot. You have to try as hard as you can to make your dreams come true."

"Is that what you did, Papa Pete?"

"It is. When you look at the Crunchy Pickle, you see a delicious restaurant. But when I look at it, I see my dream come true. A place where my hard work has made very hungry people happy for the last fifty years. I can't imagine what my life would have been like if I hadn't overcome my fear."

Wow, I never realized that restaurant meant so much to him.

"So what do you say, Hankie?" he asked. "Are you going to that audition tomorrow morning?"

It was real quiet out there on the terrace.

The only sound was me not answering.

CHAPTER 20

In case you're wondering, I showed up at the audition.

My hands were shaking. My knees were wobbling. My mouth was dry. My heart was racing.

But I was there. Ready to try.

CHAPTER 21

"**Good morning, Mr. Zipzer,**" a smiling woman in a black leotard and tights said. She was sitting behind a table in between two men on the stage of the big empty auditorium of Professional Performing Arts. "I'm Trudi Ferguson, the dance teacher here. This is Garry Marshall from our drama department, and Tom Milkus from the music area."

"You guys are teachers here?" I asked.

"Why yes," she said. "Why do you sound so surprised, Hank?"

"Because you told me all your first names. At PS 87, I don't even think our teachers have first names." They all laughed, which I thought was a good start. So I went on. "As a matter of fact, at PS 87, most of the teachers don't laugh, either."

"Well, Hank," the man named Garry Marshall said. "By the way, is Hank short for Henry?"

I nodded.

"Henry's a good name," he said. "My butcher's named Henry, and boy, does he know his way around a lamb chop."

Now it was my turn to laugh.

"Anyway, Hank," he went on, "at this school, everybody calls everybody by their first name. It stirs up the creative juices. I don't know why, it just does. Creative juices are good."

Creative juices? Wow, can you imagine old Ms. Adolf talking about her creative juices? I bet they'd be gray, if she even had any.

"So what are you going to do for your audition?" the music guy asked me. "It doesn't say here on your application what specifically your talent is."

"Well, for starters," I said, "I am great at failing in math. I'm also pretty good at failing in spelling."

"So you're a funny person," Garry Marshall said. "Funny is good."

I couldn't believe we were having this conversation. I mean, I had really relaxed and was talking to these people . . . these *teachers* . . . like I had always known them. Like they were aunts and uncles or something. Except better than aunts and uncles because they weren't telling me long stories about how root beer only cost a nickel when they were growing up.

"I'm going to do a couple of monologues that I made up," I told them. "First I'll be a bowling ball, and then I'll be an alien from the planet Zork, and if we have time, I hope you'll really like my portrayal of a fox being chased by a thundering pack of horses."

They all looked very pleased at that. If I tried even one of those monologues on Principal Love, he would have given me a lecture on how I was wasting my time and his pretending to be someone I wasn't, when I could be memorizing my roman numerals instead.

"The stage is yours," Trudi Ferguson said. "Would you like to close your eyes and take a few deep breaths to prepare yourself?"

I had never actually closed my eyes in front of people I didn't know, except the time I fell asleep on my dad's lap at a Mets game and wouldn't you know it, that was the time they decided to put me on the Jumbotron.

I closed my eyes and took a deep breath, and

thought about being a bowling ball. And guess what? It worked. I could feel my brain focusing on what I was going to say and by the time I opened my eyes, I was that bowling ball, shooting down the lane.

I don't know exactly what got into me, and I don't mean to brag, but I was on fire. Each monologue got better than the one before. I don't think I've ever told a better story. The teachers must have enjoyed it, too, because they let me get all the way to the end of the fox hunt. And when I was done, after I had escaped across the river and into the brambles, I looked up and each one of them was smiling.

"You have such a lively imagination," Trudi Ferguson said.

"And a great command of the language," Tom Milkus added.

"Plus, you're funny," said Garry Marshall. "And remember, funny is good."

He didn't have to tell me that twice, even though he did.

"Seems like you got an inner oddball thing going on," he said. "And believe it or not . . ."

"I know," I interrupted. "Oddball is good."

We all laughed like we were just hanging out at Harvey's, having a slice of pepperoni pizza. As for me, I was lapping up their compliments like Cheerio laps up his doggy delicious lamb and rice treats. Man oh man, was this ever going well.

Until my worst nightmare happened.

Tom Milkus stood up from the table, gathered a set of stapled papers in his hands, and approached me.

"You obviously have a talent for improvisation, Hank," he said. "And that is vital in the arts. However, we also need to see that you can work with written material and deliver lines from a script."

He handed me the sheets of stapled paper. I wasn't liking where this was going.

"This is a scene from a play that our students performed last year," he said. "Take a few minutes, read it over, and then come back. Garry will read the other part with you."

"You mean like now?" I asked. "As in today? Can't I take this home and work on it?"

"In the theater, this is called cold reading. It's a very important skill for an actor."

I looked down at the pages in my hand. They were filled with words, but my eyes couldn't make out one of them. They were swimming on the page like a school of tuna fish. And not in the can, either.

"Is there a problem, Hank?" Trudi Ferguson asked. "You don't look too happy."

"Oh, no problem at all, Ms. Ferguson. I mean, Trudi. I'm just going to step outside, read this over, and be right back."

I took a couple steps off the stage and turned around.

"I'll be right back," I said.

"Yeah, we know," Garry Marshall said. "You just said that."

"Good," I said. "So we're all agreed that I'll be right back."

I actually left the stage walking backward, smiling at them like everything was just fine and dandy. But I think you and I both know that for me, reading pages I haven't seen before is like flying to the moon without a rocket or a spacesuit or oxygen.

In other words, impossible.

CHAPTER 22

I stood in the hall outside the auditorium, just holding those pages, as if holding them was going to help me read them. Way down at the end of the hall, I saw my mom sipping a cup of coffee, waiting with the other parents. She waved and gave me a thumbs-up. I waved back with the hand holding the scene. At least those pages were being useful for something, because I certainly wasn't reading them.

Okay, Hank. What are you going to do? Just stand here or are you going to at least look at the paper?

I chose to look at the paper. I stared at the first word really hard. It looked familiar but I had no idea what it was. I'm not the greatest reader in the world, and when I'm nervous, I lose even the little ability I have.

Concentrate, Hank. Sound out that word.

Come on. T-H . . . what's the sound for T-H? Now add an E. Got it! THE. The first word is THE. Okay, one word down, three pages to go!

It didn't go so well after that. I tried to see those words, to be calm and apply all the sounding out skills Dr. Berger had worked with me on. But it was like they were never in my head in the first place. As I stared at the page, I realized for the first time I was walking in a circle, like Cheerio chasing his tail. No wonder I was dizzy.

Keep your eyes on that page, Hank. You've got to do this. You want to get in here, don't you? Because otherwise, it's MS 245, here you come.

Suddenly, I realized that I wasn't alone in the hall. Sitting on a bench, waiting quietly, watching me freak out, was a tall girl about my age, wearing pink tights and a tutu. I don't mean to overstate the case, but she was the most beautiful girl I'd ever seen.

"It's scary, isn't it?" she said. "I'm going in after you."

"I'm a little nervous," I said. "I didn't know I was going to have to do this."

"I'm sure you'll be great."

Sure, that's easy for her to say. She's never been inside my brain.

"I'm going to try," I said. "The one good thing is at least I don't have to do this on my toes."

She laughed and I swear, it sounded like the wind chimes on our terrace on a breezy summer day.

Wow. Did I just think that? I must be coming completely unglued.

"You're funny," she said.

"Funny is good," I answered.

We both laughed, and for a minute, I completely forgot where I was and everything was back to normal. Then Trudi Ferguson stuck her head out of the big double doors, and where I was came into focus really quickly.

"We're ready for you, Hank," she said. "Looking forward to hear what you've prepared."

"So am I," I said, and the beautiful dancer laughed along with us.

As I followed Trudi through the door and up onto the stage where the other two teachers were waiting for me, I only had one thought.

Run.

Run for the hills. Run for home. Run for cover.

It doesn't matter where you run, just get out of there.

But I didn't run. I stood my ground.

"Are you ready to begin?" Garry Marshall asked me. "I'll read the first line, and then you just jump right in."

"I got my jumping shoes on," I said.

Garry cleared his throat and began.

"Howdy there, Sheriff Jed. You're looking mighty dressed up today in them new boots."

He paused, waiting for me to say my line. I knew it started with THE, but THE what? The boots? The horses? The stage coach?

My mind was racing, and I tried to make my eyes stay on the page and do their work.

Come on, boys. Look at that second word. You got to help me out here.

"The circus is coming to town, Jethro. So I dressed up."

Garry looked confused as he flipped through all three pages.

"Excuse me, Hank," he said. "I don't see that

line anywhere. Do you have a different script?"

"Actually, Garry, yes I do."

"That's strange," he said. "How did that happen?"

Many explanations raced through my mind. I met a jolly old elf in the hall and he snatched my original script and replaced it with this one. The place is crawling with elves, you know. Or how about this: The spirit of William Shakespeare visited me with his quill pen and dictated an entirely new play that he thought was better. You know that Shakespeare, he likes it to be done his way, and there's just no arguing with him.

While I was deciding which story to tell, a funny thing happened.

I told the truth.

I didn't exactly decide to, but when I looked at those three nice people, I just couldn't hide who I really was.

"The truth is," I heard myself saying. "I really want to come here. You guys are so great and I just loved rehearsing for this audition and feeling so creative and special. But I can't read out loud. In fact, I can't read very well at all unless I concentrate with all my brain and even then, it's really hard for me. I have learning challenges that have always made school difficult so you might as well know that right now because if I did come here, I probably couldn't keep up, anyway, although I really want to keep up but I just never seem to be able to."

Wow. That came out in a big gush. And guess what? I wasn't finished.

"It's pretty frustrating feeling like you're smart inside but when you try to get it outside, everything just gets all tangled up. It makes me feel like my brain is caught in a spider web, and try as I might, I just can't ever escape from it. People always think I'm not trying hard enough, but they don't have any idea how hard I really do try."

"Hank," Trudi Ferguson said. "Why didn't you tell us?"

"Because I really want to be a student here and I'm sure, with everyone in the whole city that you have to choose from, the last person you're going to want is a guy with learning challenges."

I could feel myself starting to cry, that feeling

when your throat tightens up and your voice starts to squeak like a mouse. I sure didn't want them to see that.

"So thank you so much for your time and for being so cool and letting me call you by your first names and everything, and I'll just send the next person in. By the way, she's a ballerina and I'll bet she's really great."

Without waiting for their answer, I turned and ran out of the room as fast as I could. As I came crashing through the double doors into the hall, the beautiful ballerina smiled at me and said, "How'd it go?"

"Fine," I squeaked. "Your turn."

All I knew was that I had to hold the tears back until I was out on the street. I was able to do that, but when I hit the sidewalk, boy oh boy oh boy, did they ever come fast and furious.

CHAPTER 23

My mom was really nice on the way home. She tried every trick in the book to make me feel better, including an offer to stop at Harvey's for a slice of pizza, or even two slices if I wanted. Nothing worked, though. I felt like I had blown my best chance at ever having a good time in school, and my whole future was going to be more spelling tests and Nick McKelty blowing his bad breath into my face.

When we got home, Emily and my Dad were playing electronic scrabble. My dad barely looked up from the game. I guess he was working on a seven letter word with triple points, which is the kind of thing that needs his full attention.

"How'd it go?" Emily asked, taking a break from the game.

"Let's just say," I said, really not wanting to go into details, "that if I were a submarine,

I would be at the bottom of the ocean, below where the clams live."

"Honestly, Hank. Even you should know the clam cannot survive in that depth of water."

"Actually, Em, I don't know that. And do you know why? Because I'm a stupid guy who can't read a bunch of simple words off a page. So if you'll excuse me now, I'm going to live the rest of my life in my room."

I walked into my room for a good sulk, but I couldn't even do that. Baby Harry was at it again, and my room had the unmistakable aroma of strained peas. He was a talented kid when it came to the filled diaper department. At least one of the Zipzer boys was good at something.

Ashley and Frankie tried their best to cheer me up. We spent the rest of the day in our basement clubhouse, with them telling me what a cool guy I was and me not hearing a word they said.

Thank goodness there was a Mets game on TV on Sunday, because by that time, I was starting to bore myself. I don't know about you, but I can only be in a bad mood for about a day and a half before I need a Mets game and some microwave popcorn with Junior Mints dropped into it while the popcorn is still hot so that the chocolate melts and makes a delicious, gooey mess.

On Monday, Nick McKelty was particularly obnoxious at school. Right before lunch, he grabbed all my Number Two pencils and broke them in half, for no reason.

"This is perfect, Zipperbutt," he said, handing them back to me. "You're short, and now you got short pencils, just like you."

It took me all of lunch to figure out how to get him back, but finally I came up with a brilliant plan. I used two halves of one of my broken pencils like chopsticks, and picked up one of Luke Whitman's already-been-used nose tissues. Being very careful not to let any part of my body make contact with it, I carried the disgusting thing back to class and carefully slipped it in to McKelty's sweatshirt pocket. When he stuck his stubby hands in there on the way home from school, he was going to get a delightfully slimy surprise.

I thought that was going to be the highlight of my day, but boy, did I have a surprise waiting for me when I got home.

"This letter came for you today," my mom said the minute I walked into the apartment.

I don't get many letters. Actually, I don't get any letters except a card on my birthday from my aunt Maxine. I really like that letter because it always has a crisp ten dollar bill in it. I held up this letter to the light to see if there was a ten dollar bill in it. No such luck.

"Why don't you read it to me, Mom? It's probably someone wanting me to subscribe to *Highlights for Children*."

"I don't think so," my mom said, "because the return address is from the Professional Performing Arts School."

"Oh great. I get to find out a second time that I didn't get in."

My mom opened the envelope and pulled out the letter.

"Dear Hank," she read. "It was a real pleasure for the three of us to meet you. We really enjoyed your imagination and your positive spirit. We've talked over your application with the entire admissions committee at great length. And we feel that if you agree to work on the academic areas that are difficult for you, such as cold reading, then we are happy to offer you a spot in the middle school class starting this September."

I couldn't believe what I was hearing.

"Mom, could you check the name at the top of the letter and see if it's really addressed to *Hank* Zipzer. Maybe there was another Zipzer who applied."

"Honey, it says your name right here. This letter is for you. It's signed by Trudi, Garry, and Tom. And wait, there's a handwritten note at the bottom. It's from Garry and it says, 'Funny is good. Welcome, Hank.'"

At first I couldn't say one word. I just stood there letting the words in that letter wash over me. Finally, they must have sunk as far as they were going to go into my brain, and I just exploded.

"I GOT IN!" I said, over and over again. "I'm in! I was accepted! They want me to come there! I was accepted! I can't believe it! Mom, can you believe it? I got in! I got in! I got in!"

CHAPTER 24

It took me less than forty seconds to race to the telephone.

"Who are you calling, honey?" my mom asked.

"I'm calling the school to say yes, before they change their mind."

"Do you think you might need the phone number?" she said, holding the letter up.

"Another brilliant suggestion from the Mom department! Reel it off to me."

She did just that, saying the numbers in quick succession. My dialing finger did not budge.

"Oh, mom-o," I said. "Remember, it's me, Hank. I need one number at a time, really slowly."

"I'm so sorry, honey. I wasn't thinking."

It seemed like the ringing on the other end went on forever until someone finally picked up the phone. I didn't ask who it was, I just blurted out, "Yes!"

The man on the other end said, "Excuse me?"

"This is Hank Zipzer, and yes, I accept."

He laughed.

"I think you want the office," he said. "They're already closed for the day. I'm William, the custodian, but here everyone calls me Tiny which by the way, I'm not."

"Nice to meet you, Tiny," I said. "I'm going to be a student there in the fall, so I'll get to meet you in person."

"You sound like a nice kid, Hank. Congratulations on getting in."

When I hung up, I felt like a million bucks. Everyone at that school was so nice and welcoming.

As soon as I got off the phone, my mom suggested that we should have a family meeting to tell my dad and Emily the good news. Emily was really glad for me, although Katherine expressed some negative feelings. At least, I think they were negative feelings. I don't know iguana speak, but I'm pretty sure when her tongue shot out and she hissed into my face for twenty seconds, she wasn't asking me to dance.

My dad's reaction was a little more complicated. He was half mad, half glad, and half doubtful. I know that's too many halves, but that's the way I saw his reaction.

"Look, Hank. You know this artsy school wouldn't be my first choice for you, but if you're so sure of it, go ahead and give it a try."

"I'm going to work really hard there, Dad."

"Well, that would be a nice change, wouldn't it? Meanwhile, congratulations."

That didn't exactly feel like the way congratulations should feel, but knowing my dad, it was the best I was going to get.

"Hank," my mom said. "Why don't you walk over to Papa Pete's apartment and tell him the good news."

"Why don't I just call him?"

"I think it would be really nice for you to give him this news in person. And here's an idea. Why don't you stay at Papa Pete's and do your homework there, and we'll meet you at the Crunchy Pickle for a little family dinner."

"Do I have to order soylami, or can I get a real pastrami sandwich?" I asked.

"Well, this is a special occasion so real meat it is."

Just then, Katherine hissed again.

"And no, Madame Iguana, you can't have a bite. It's my pastrami, not yours."

"Iguanas are primarily herbivores, Hank. Don't you know anything?"

"Yes, Emily, I do. I know that I'm going to Professional Performing Arts. And in the future, I'd prefer that you keep your insults, put downs, and other rude remarks to yourself."

"Okay, I'll call Robert and insult him. He doesn't mind."

I took my book bag and jacket and said good-bye to Cheerio. I don't think he actually understood what was going on, which makes sense, because dogs don't really go to middle school, as far as I know. But he could sense something good was going on, because he gave me extra licks on my way out.

When I got to Papa Pete's and told him the news, he started to cry.

"What's wrong, Papa Pete?" I asked him.

"What's wrong? Everything is right! I knew you could do this. You were so worried and look what you've accomplished. I am overjoyed for you, and so proud of you, young man, that my buttons are popping off my shirt."

Then he swept me up in his big, strong arms and gave me the bear hug of all time.

And then a surprising thing happened. I started to cry, too, which took me by total surprise. I don't know where those tears came from . . . maybe from I'm-the-Happiest-Kid-on-the-Planet-Land. But they just came pouring out. And there we were, Papa Pete and me, hugging like there was no tomorrow.

CHAPTER 25

Two hours later, when I pushed open the glass door to the Crunchy Pickle, it was alive with energy. Everyone I knew was there. As I walked in, they all screamed, "Hooray for Hank!" and started clapping. I started clapping, too.

I looked over at my mom, who was smiling at me from behind the meat counter, where she was making sandwiches alongside Carlos and Vlady.

"I thought a party was pretty necessary," she said.

Then I saw Frankie and Ashley, who came running up to me and jumped on me like I had just hit a home run in the World Series. We wound up in a heap on the floor, and before I knew it, we went from a pile of three to a pile of five when Luke Whitman and Ryan Shimozato decided to join in.

"You pulled off a great one," Luke said,

spraying saliva in my face. I didn't even care about his spitting problem because I knew he didn't mean to be gross.

Ryan didn't say anything. He just kept pounding me on the top of my head, which I think means congratulations. It was fun at first, and then I finally said, "Come on, guys. Get off me. You're squishing my stomach."

"How cool are you, Zip," Frankie said.

"Very cool," I answered. "I knew I'd get in all along."

"Right, and my name is Bernice," Frankie said.

"I am so happy for you, Hank," Ashley said. "I've decided I'm going to rhinestone a baseball cap for you that says P.P.A.S."

"P.P.A.S.?" I asked. "What does that spell?"

"Earth to Hank. It's the initials of the school you're going to . . . as in Professional Performing Arts School."

"Right," I said. "I knew that."

"Yeah, and his name is Bernice," she answered, pointing to Frankie.

The three of us cracked up, just like we'd been doing since preschool.

Before I knew it, Frankie and Ashley jumped up on the seat of one of the turquoise booths. Frankie picked up his glass of apricot-mango juice and called for everyone's attention.

"Ladies and gentlemen, boys and girls, and children of all ages," he called out. I remember hearing a ringmaster say that at the circus when we were little. He always loved it.

"Ashley and I would like to propose a toast to our best friend, Hank 'I'm Going Places' Zipzer. You did it, pal. You're on your way!"

"Let's hear it for Hank," Ashley chimed in.

As I looked around the room, I saw almost everyone I knew raising their apricot-mango juice glasses toward me. I mean, everyone. There was Mr. Rock, who shot me a big thumbs-up. And Dr. Berger who looked so proud. Mrs. Fink, who had finally changed out of her bathrobe for the occasion, winked at me. And even the girls from school were there, Kim Paulson and Katie Sperling and my good friend Heather Payne.

Suddenly, Robert Upchurch, Emily's pencil-neck boyfriend, jumped up to join Frankie and Ashley on the booth seat. Of course, he fell off immediately because he is such a skinny weakling and Frankie had to pull him out from under the table. When he finally regained his balance and stood up on the booth again, he cleared his throat, which sounded like he had been keeping a small hippopotamus hidden in there, and spoke to the crowd.

"If I could just say a few words," he began.

"Keep it to a very few, Upchurch," Ryan called out and everyone laughed because if there's one thing Robert Upchurch can't do, it's say a short sentence.

"My first memory of Hank is when I was in kindergarten and he was in first grade," he began. "He was eating a tuna fish sandwich in the lunchroom, and I wanted it so badly but I couldn't eat it because I'm allergic to mayonnaise."

"Sit down, Upchurch," Ryan called out.

I jumped up on the booth to join Robert. I knew he was trying his best to make a good speech, but the guy just couldn't get out of his own mucous.

"That was very touching, Robert," I interrupted, helping him down off the booth seat so he wouldn't fall flat on his face again. "And speaking of touching, I am so touched that you all came to my party tonight. It's a big day for me and I want to thank you for helping me achieve this very important goal."

I looked out into the faces, and saw Dr. and Mrs. Townsend and the good Doctors Wong smiling at me. Gosh, they had known me since I was a tiny baby. I couldn't imagine having grown up without them.

"Some people told me that I would never be a success in school," I went on, surprising myself that I was actually making a speech. "But for the first time in my whole life, I feel like I can succeed. I really think the Professional Performing Arts School is the place for me and you're all invited to my first performance next year. But right now, it's pastrami time. What do you say, folks? Let's eat."

It was a perfect night. I mean, think about it. I had all my friends there cheering for me. I felt really proud of what I had accomplished. And I had stuffed in as much pastrami and brown mustard as my stomach could hold.

What more could a guy want?

CHAPTER 26

The next morning, I couldn't wait to get to school. I was up way before my clock radio was. Maybe for the first time in history, I was raring to get to school, because today was the day I was going to let Ms. Adolf know that everything she had ever thought about me was dead wrong. She had said to me so many times that I was never going to make something of myself that I almost started to believe it. But even though she couldn't teach me to spell or to do long division, Ms. Adolf did teach me a really important lesson which is that you have to believe in yourself and not believe what all the adults are saying about you if your feelings way down deep tell you they're wrong. You know you the best.

By seven o'clock, I was standing at the door with my sweatshirt already zipped and my backpack slung over one shoulder. The only problem was, I don't even leave until eight.

My dad came out of his bedroom, still in his pajama bottoms and T-shirt, and headed toward the kitchen. It was his turn to put out breakfast for Emily and me. When he saw me standing at the door, all dressed and ready to go, he said, "Are you real or am I dreaming you? I've never seen you up this early and ready to go unless we were going to a theme park or a Mets game."

"That's because what I'm doing today is going to be even more fun than hanging upside down on the Cyclone Double Loop."

"I like to hear that attitude about school," my father said. "That's what you should have been thinking all along."

For a minute, I had forgotten that I can't have this kind of conversation with my dad. He likes to turn every single thing into a lesson, even down to the right way to eat a black-and-white cookie. He doesn't approve of my technique, which is to try to get some chocolate and vanilla icing in every bite, so they can mix in my mouth. He says it's messy and unnecessary. Folks, I'm talking heaven and he says it's foolish.

While I was waiting for the next hour to pass,

I decided to take my acceptance letter out of my backpack and read it over and over again. I think we all know that I have real trouble reading anything cold right off the page. And since I was planning to read the letter aloud to Ms. Adolf, I wanted to get it perfect. Besides, I could never get tired of hearing those two great words, "Welcome, Hank!"

I was too excited to wait until eight o'clock to leave, so I called Frankie and Ashley and told them I'd meet them in class. I got to school in record time, and by the time I reached the steps, I was out of breath. Even with that, I still had to fight the urge to shout my good news up and down the halls of every floor. It was there on my tongue, ready to shoot out of my mouth at any second. I didn't have to wait long, because the first person I ran into running up the stairs was none other than Principal Leland Love.

"Walk, young man," he said. "Where are you going in such a hurry?"

"I'm so glad you asked, Principal Love. Actually, I am going to the Professional Performing Arts School. In the fall, that is. They accepted me."

Wow, you could have knocked him over with a feather. Even the Statue of Liberty mole on his cheek looked surprised.

"Well," he said. "That must make you feel very special."

"As a matter of fact, it does."

"Excellent. That is what education is intended to do . . . to guide you down life's ever winding path in a sure-footed way."

Oh boy. I could feel it coming on. The old Principal Love speech-a-roony. I sure wasn't going to miss those at my new middle school. But he was on a roll, and I knew there was no stopping him, so I settled in for the lecture.

"Now what's important for you to remember here, Hank, is that the path presented to you is the one you need to stay on. There will be many paths leading off the main path, and you should not be tempted to take any of them. You may find many obstacles along the path, let's call them boulders, and you must find a way to step over them without stubbing your toe."

"Don't you worry about that, Principal Love. I'm getting a new pair of shoes before school starts."

"Yes, of course. Good idea. Now . . . just remember this. As you trudge down life's path, keep your head up, your eyes forward, your throat cleared, and your walking stick handy."

"I'm going to write that down as soon as I get to my classroom," I said. "And hang it up over my desk at home."

Principal Love seemed pretty pleased with that and with our conversation in general, so I used that as an opportunity to skedaddle out of there. Knowing him, that life path lecture could have gone on all summer. And I had a very important thing left to do upstairs.

As I walked up the stairs, it suddenly occurred to me that my days of walking up these steps that I knew so well were coming to an end. I wondered what I would think if I ever came back here after I was all grown up. Hmmm. The first thing I'd think was that there was a lot of chewing gum stuck on the back side of the railing. And then, I'd probably think that these stairs led me to Ms. Adolf's classroom, two years in a row . . . lucky me . . . which was always a really difficult place for me.

She was sitting at her desk, red pencil in

hand, grading papers. That must be her favorite thing to do, since she seems to spend twenty-four hours a day doing it.

"Hi, Ms. Adolf," I said. "Am I disturbing you?"

"Only slightly," she answered without even looking up from her desk. "What is it, Henry?"

Wow, a second ago, I had been feeling on top of the world. Now, I was feeling unbelievably nervous. That woman could pop a balloon without a pin.

"I just wanted to share with you . . . well, actually, read a letter to . . . that I thought you might really like."

"If you must," she said, taking off her gray glasses and staring at me with her gray eyes. "And what does this letter say that is so important?"

I cleared my throat, stood as tall as I was ever going to get, and started reading.

"Dear Hank. It was a real pleasure for—"

She stopped me mid-sentence and held out her gray hand.

"Let me see that letter, please," she said.

I handed it to her, but I was still in shock. She

didn't even let me get the first sentence out. And, I had practiced all morning.

She read the letter without saying a word, but I noticed that her eyebrows went up in surprise, but just for a moment. I took a breath, waiting for her to respond. Would she say, "Congratulations"? Or would she say, "I'm happy for you, Hank"? Or maybe she'd say, "You finally did it, Hank."

None of that came out of her mouth. Instead, she swooped up her red pencil, and started marking up the letter.

"Who are these people?" she said. "Definitely not educators of any reputation. They left out two commas, a period, and a capital letter at the beginning of the third sentence."

I know. You think I'm kidding. But I'M NOT.

That gray faced woman sat there correcting my acceptance letter with a big, fat, great cloud hanging over her gray bun.

"Ms. Adolf, may I have my letter back, please? I'd like to read you just one sentence from it because you might have missed it. Here . . . it says, we loved your imagination and positive spirit, and we are *happy* to offer you a spot in our middle school class."

"Well, I hope when you get there, you remind those free-spirited people that the English language has rules, and commas are an important part of those rules."

"Ms. Adolf, they are really good teachers there. They know all about my learning challenges, and they still want me. They looked at all of me, not just where I put my commas."

"Then it sounds like you and they will be a perfect match."

With that, she stood up and walked toward me. I had no idea what she was about to do. She reached out to me and touched my shoulder, and then she touched the other one. And then, she gave me the stiffest, boniest, grayest hug I'd ever received in my entire life.

"Good luck to you, young man," she said. Then she turned, sat down at her desk, picked up her red pencil and went back to work.

She never looked up again.

THREE MONTHS LATER... FIRST DAY OF MIDDLE SCHOOL

At seven o'clock in the morning on a Monday in September, Frankie, Ashley, and I met in the lobby. That was normal. We all had our new backpacks for the first day of school. That was normal. Then we headed down 78th Street toward Broadway, in the opposite direction of PS 87. That was not normal. That was brand-new.

When we reached the stop for the Broadway bus, I turned to them and didn't know exactly what to say.

"So . . . this is where I wait for my bus," I finally said.

"Our subway stop is one block up," Frankie pointed out.

We were all quiet for a minute. This was the first time in our whole lives we weren't going to school together.

"You're going to be so great, Hank," Ashley said, all of a sudden throwing her arms around me.

"Zip, you're going to wow them," Frankie added, joining in our three-way hug.

We just stood there holding on for a minute, like we were in a football huddle. We might have stood there forever, but my bus arrived, and the hiss of the doors opening told me it was time to go.

"We're still going to meet after school, right?" I hollered out to them as I climbed aboard.

"The clubhouse," Frankie shouted back. "Four o'clock."

Ashley shouted something, too, but I couldn't hear her because the bus doors slammed shut when she was still in mid-sentence.

"Put your money in the slot, son, and take a seat," the driver said to me.

I did. And as I turned to find a seat, I saw a sea of faces looking at me. I don't know where I got the nerve, but suddenly I blurted out, "Hi, everyone. We haven't met, but we're going to see each other a lot, because I'll be taking this bus to the Professional Performing Arts School.

Today's my first day. I'm Hank Zipzer, by the way."

To my surprise, some of the passengers answered back.

"Hi, Hank," a couple of them called out. "Good luck today."

I took a seat by the window. All summer, I had been practicing taking the bus with my mother, so I knew the bus-related rules like that you had to have exact change and ring a buzzer to let the driver know you were getting off at the next stop. But what I had never practiced was being all alone on the bus. That was new, too.

As I looked out the window, I watched my neighborhood pass by—all the familiar buildings that I knew inside and out. It felt really strange to be leaving them, but it was exciting, too. I mean, I was doing what adults do. That could only mean one thing. I was growing up.

Passing the corner of 77th and Broadway on our way downtown, I saw a bunch of kids walking to their new middle school, MS 245, including many of my friends from Ms. Adolf's class. And wouldn't you know it, Nick McKelty, being the Tick he is, was reaching his grimy thick hand into Ryan Shimozato's backpack and pulling out the dessert from his lunch bag.

It's what he does best, I thought. Some things just never change. I myself felt very changed.

As we drove on, my neighborhood drifted into new neighborhoods with stores and movie theaters and skyscrapers that I had only been to a few times. As we approached 48th Street, I pushed the buzzer to let the driver know I wanted to get off. As the doors hissed open and I turned to leave, I waved at everyone and shouted, "Nice riding with you."

It was great to hear the people on the bus laugh, and to know that I still had it—the old Zipzer attitude.

There was a big sign hanging above the front door of my new school that said, "WELCOME STUDENTS!"

"Thank you very much," I whispered to myself. "I feel welcome."

The truth is, I felt a lot of other things, too: Scared because it was all new to me. Shy because these were all new people. And short because I am.

I walked into the lobby and just stood there

for a minute, realizing I had no idea where to go. Before I had time to panic, Trudi Ferguson came up to me in her black leotard with a clipboard in her hand.

"Welcome, Hank. Glad to see you here. Your first period class is Language Arts with Garry Marshall. It's in Room 4C, up two flights, first door on your left."

First problem solved. Now I knew where I was going. This middle school thing was turning out to be not so hard after all.

The only thing I didn't know was which direction was left. But I figured it out when I got upstairs by poking my head in the rooms on both sides of the hall until I saw Mr. Marshall.

Uh-oh. I forgot. I have to call him Garry.

Can you imagine if I had called Ms. Adolf Fanny? First of all, I would have cracked myself up just saying the word Fanny. And second of all, she would have put me in detention until I had a beard down to my knees.

I took a seat in class. The seats were arranged in a horseshoe shape, not in rows like I was used to at my other school. The first thing I noticed was that when we were sitting like that, you could see everybody's face. That was a good idea. I wasn't going to have to spend three years looking at the hairs on the back of the neck of the kid in front of me.

The other students all seemed nice, and a little nervous, just like me. When the bell rang, Garry welcomed us all to his class.

"We're going to be examining creativity in here," he said, "which I believe is as necessary to human beings as food and water. Think of creativity as a great cheeseburger for the soul."

"I'll have two of those," the kid next to me in a bowling shirt with his name over the pocket called out. I'd tell you his name, but of course, I couldn't read the letters. I was surprised that the kid just shouted out his comment without raising his hand. And I was even more surprised that Garry didn't seem to mind.

"Now, who thinks they know what creativity is?" Garry said, leaning against one of the empty desks.

"I feel creative when I play the drums," one of the boys commented. I could have guessed that because he was wearing a T-shirt that had a picture of a drum set on it.

"Drumming is good," Garry answered, "and I'm happy for you. But does anyone here know what creativity is?"

I raised my hand because that's what I was used to.

"Ahh, Hank," he said. "Let's hear what you have to say."

"I think creativity is when you let your feelings swirl around in your brain and then let them explode out of you in a way that can only come from you."

Garry paused for a long time. I didn't know if that was good or bad, if my answer was right or wrong.

"You know something, Hank," he said at last. "You are really smart. And smart is good."

Smart? No teacher had ever said that before. Wow.

This *was* a brand-new me!

About the Authors

Henry Winkler is an actor, producer, director, coauthor, public speaker, husband, father, brother, uncle, and godfather. He lives in Los Angeles with his wife, Stacey. They have three children named Jed, Zoe, and Max, and three dogs named Monty, Charlotte, and Linus. He is so proud of the Hank Zipzer series that he could scream—which he does sometimes, in his backyard!

If you gave him two words to describe how he feels about the Hank Zipzer series, he would say: "I am thrilled that Lin Oliver is my partner and we write all these books together." Yes, you're right, that was sixteen words. But, hey! He's got learning challenges.

Lin Oliver is a writer and producer of movies, books, and television series for children and families. She has created over one hundred episodes of television, four movies, and over twelve books. She lives in Los Angeles with her husband, Alan. They have three sons named Theo, Ollie, and Cole, and a very adorable but badly behaved puppy named Dexter.

If you gave her two words to describe this book, she would say "funny and compassionate." If you asked her what compassionate meant, she would say "full of kindness." She would not make you look it up in the dictionary.